The Wallflower

By Dana Marie Bell

Is Emma ready for a bite?

A *Hunting Love* story, *Halle Puma* Series Book 1.

Emma Carter has been in love with Max Cannon since high school, but he barely knew she existed. Now she runs her own unique curio shop, and she's finally come out of her shell and into her own.

When Max returns to his small hometown to take up his duties as the Halle Pride's Alpha, he finds that shy little Emma has grown up. That small spark of something he'd always felt around the teenager has blossomed into something more—his mate!

Taking her "out for a bite" ensures that the luscious Emma will be permanently his.

But Max's ex has plans of her own. Plans that don't include Emma being around to interfere. To keep her Alpha, Emma must prove to the Pride that she has what it takes to be Max's mate.

Warning: This title contains explicit sex, graphic language, loads of giggles and a hot, blond Alpha male.

Treasure Hunting

By J. B. McDonald

Can love tame a jaguar god?

A *Hunting Love* story.

A good tromp through the jungle fending off giant bugs and hunting for long-lost ruins in South America is exactly Meg's idea of a great vacation. She takes the sudden appearance of a wounded jaguar in stride, thinking it'll make an interesting story. But when she wakes up to find a man in place of a cat, she wonders who's going to believe it!

Santiago has learned the hard way that he and human women just don't mix. When you can change into an animal at will, it tends to upset people. But despite his best intentions, he finds himself falling hard for the little blonde who saved his life.

It'll take a leap of faith—and of love. Or this treasure will slip through his fingers.

Warning: This work contains graphic m/f sex, bad language, and terrible humor.

Hunting Love

A Samhain Publishing, Ltd. publication.

Samhain Publishing, Ltd.
577 Mulberry Street, Suite 1520
Macon, GA 31201
www.samhainpublishing.com

Hunting Love
Print ISBN: 978-1-60504-106-3

Editing by Angela James
Cover by Anne Cain

The Wallflower, 1-59998- 918-2
First Samhain Publishing, Ltd. electronic publication: April 2008
Treasure Hunting, 1-59998- 920-4
First Samhain Publishing, Ltd. electronic publication: April 2008
First Samhain Publishing, Ltd. print publication: March 2009

Contents

The Wallflower

Dana Marie Bell

Dedication

To Mom, for always helping me look on the bright side and cheering me on even when you weren't certain you knew what you were cheering about.

To Dad, who grinned so wide I thought his face would crack when he heard I was going to be published. Yes, I promise I'll write a fantasy story one day, just don't expect me to leave out the romance.

To my grandmother, who's read every word I've ever written and loved it even when we both knew it sucked. I love you, Memom!

To my husband, Dusty; you've made all my dreams come true. (Other than the cabana boy one. But that's okay. You're not getting your big-breasted masseuse either, so we're even.) Thank you for believing in me. I love you, sweetheart.

Special thanks to A and BR for reading this, helping me fix it and polish it up, and for cheering with me when I got the contract. Also thanks to JG and JW for the technical assistance.

Prologue

"So, have you heard? Max is back." Marie watched with a friendly smile as Emma carefully wrapped her purchase. Emma felt her heart give a little jump at the news, though it wasn't the first time she'd heard it. The knowledge that the hunky Dr. Cannon had moved back home for good after ten years away was hot gossip to all the women who trooped through her store.

Marie Howard was there to pick up a hand-crafted mirror with beautiful hand-painted tiles. Livia was there, even though she hated both Emma and Becky, because she was friends with Marie. As far as Livia was concerned, they were directly responsible for her breakup with Max.

Livia Patterson was one of the town beauties and knew it. Fine boned with alabaster skin, she had just the right dusting of rose at her cheeks to set off her pale blonde perfection. Add blue eyes the color of forget-me-nots and a tall, wispy build, and she was the epitome of the fragile blonde. The woman could brawl like a linebacker when the time came; she could shriek, and bats for miles around fell dead to the ground; but man if she didn't work the whole Penelope Pitstop thing, and men fell for it. They loved that whole delicate flower of womanhood crap she managed to pull off so flawlessly. Not that Emma envied her or anything. Not really.

Men looked at Emma and saw sturdy womanhood. Hips made for birthing, plain brown eyes and nondescript brown hair, at five-foot-two inches Emma would never, literally, be able to stand up to Livia. Add in the fact that most of the town thought she was in a gay relationship with Becky and her social calendar remained depressingly empty.

"Apparently Max is planning on taking over Dr. Brewster's practice; he and Adrian will be partners," Livia cooed.

"So you've already spoken to him?" Marie's expression of polite curiousness didn't quite mesh with her tone of voice. Emma didn't dare look too closely, but she thought Marie was almost exasperated with her friend. Everyone knew how hard Livia had once chased Max. Maybe she thought she could get the old fires burning once again?

"Yes, Max just bought his parents' old house. I can't wait to get in there and redecorate." Emma could practically see Livia rubbing her hands in anticipation. "Of course, nothing in this shop will do. No real craftsman things. I want genuine antiques, not knock-offs." Livia's contemptuous gaze raked the store, and its owner, with equal derision.

When Livia's back was turned, Emma, in a fit of childishness, mimicked the blonde as closely as possible. Marie wound up choking on a sip of tea as Emma put her hand on her hip and mouthed along with Livia's words. "Of course, everyone knows Max would never set foot inside Wallflowers. Does he even know you exist, Emma?"

Emma tapped her nail on her chin thoughtfully as Livia turned back to her. "Yes, actually, I believe he does. Something…something to do with…punch. Cherry punch, if I recall correctly." That had been the incident that broke up Max and Livia; Becky had spilled cherry punch all over Livia's white prom dress in retaliation for some comment of Livia's concerning Emma. Max had, apparently, taken Emma and Becky's side and had broken off his relationship with Livia. Livia had hated Emma and Becky ever since. Emma was pretty sure Livia was the one who kept the whole gay couple rumor alive.

The look on the blonde's face was filled with hatred until she smoothed it out, once again the cool, delicate woman most of Halle knew. She smiled at Emma with pity. "I hear Jimmy left town recently. What's wrong, Emma, didn't he like sharing you with Becky? Or perhaps you couldn't talk her into a ménage a trois?"

Emma smiled back, hiding the hurt over Jimmy with practiced ease. They'd known before he left that their relationship wasn't going anywhere, and it wasn't Jimmy's fault. "So you've been invited to Max's housewarming party?" Sometimes it helped to have friends in odd places; Max's best friend had become one of her best artisans and closest friends. He'd made Marie's mirror and supplied quite a bit of glass wall art for the store.

Livia's eyes flickered; she knew nothing about the party. Emma mentally chalked up a score on her mental scoreboard. On the downside, Emma hadn't been invited either, not that she'd expected to be.

"That party is supposed to be a surprise." Livia waved her hand airily. Emma merely raised an amused eyebrow, not deceived in the least. "Oh, well, hopefully you won't spill the beans to Max. Oh, wait. When, exactly, was the last time *you* spoke to Max?" Livia smiled coldly.

Emma clapped in mock approval. "Wow, Livia. Way to express your inner twelve year old."

Grinding her teeth on a fake smile, Livia turned to Marie. "I'll wait for you outside. The atmosphere in here is so cloying and sweet. I really don't know how you can stand it." She stepped outside and sat on the bench Emma and Becky had put out front, looking dainty and sweet as she waved hello to her friends and acquaintances.

"Sorry about that, Emma. I forgot how much she dislikes you."

Emma turned and looked at Marie's apologetic face. She grinned. "It's no problem, Marie. If she actually came in here to buy something I'd take great pleasure in charging her double."

Marie laughed just as Becky stuck her head out of the curtained-off back room. "Has the wicked witch ridden off on her broomstick yet?"

Emma waved towards the picture window. "Not quite. She's flying our bench at the moment."

Becky carried out the mirror with a sigh. "Here you go, Marie. Hope you and Jamie like it."

"Oh, I'm sure we will," Marie replied, her eyes glued to the boxed-up mirror. She paid, chatting quietly with Becky and Emma, then left the store with a cheery wave. The two women could see her giving Livia something of a hard time as they crossed the street, but quickly lost sight of them.

"So. Max is back in town." Becky leaned back against the counter, obviously hiding a grin.

"Yup."

"You going to make a play for Dr. Yummy? I mean, since you've had a crush on him since, what, grade school?"

"Given half a chance? Maaaybe."

The two women looked at each other and laughed; they both knew Emma didn't stand a chance in hell of catching Max Cannon's attention. She hadn't done it in high school, and she certainly hadn't changed all that much since.

What would a man like Max want with someone like her?

Chapter One

"God, he is *so* fucking hot."

Emma Carter looked out the front window of Wallflowers and watched the most bodacious backside it had ever been her pleasure to see saunter down the street. Said backside was encased in a pair of tight blue jeans, causing many a female to send a prayer of thanks heavenward for the makers of Levi's. Sunlight gleamed on his golden blond hair, hair that brushed his wide shoulders, just long enough to make a stubby ponytail. Even under the bulky leather jacket you could tell he was built, his body muscular without being a temple to the god Steroid. And he had the brightest, clearest blue eyes in the state, not that she got to look at them often. He usually had them trained on someone else, like one of the sleek, beautiful women who flocked around him all the time. God, he was gorgeous. His face was almost too beautiful to be real; the only thing that marred his perfection was a small scar just along one side of his nose, barely noticeable unless you looked for it. When he spoke to her, which hadn't happened in more years than she cared to count, Emma kept her eyes trained on that scar.

When the finest ass in the world turned the corner, Emma and Becky leaned back with identical sighs. "All I want for Christmas is a piece of that." Becky sighed again, her green eyes gleaming with laughter. Her untamable brown curls danced around her head in wild abandon as she shook herself all over like a wet dog. Becky was too thin, bones showing through at wrist and ankle, and if Emma didn't know for a fact that she ate like a horse she'd have worried she was anorexic. But Becky had been cursed with a metabolism that just wouldn't quit, forcing her to eat more than most people just to maintain her weight. Emma had the opposite problem. The best that could be said about her figure was Marilyn Monroe had also been a size twelve. No matter what she did, Emma couldn't seem to drop weight. Neither woman envied the other.

"What, not a piece of Simon Holt?"

Becky blushed bright red. Dark-haired, dark-eyed, sinfully handsome Simon had featured in more than one of Becky's drunken fantasies. Emma slicked a hand through her hair. "As for me, Max Cannon could be naked and tied up with a bow under my Christmas tree and the first thing he'd probably say is, 'Hi, Edna, right? Could you untie this please? I have a date tonight'."

Both women looked at each other and giggled, then got back to work.

Emma was so proud of what she and Becky had accomplished. Friends since grade school, both women had been wallflowers. Boys didn't go for the frizzy, too-skinny Becky Yaeger or chunky, dull Emma Carter. Especially when there were girls like Livia Patterson and Belinda Campbell, both beautiful, blonde cheerleader types, around.

Both Becky and Emma had decided to go to the local college and major in business, while a number of people, including Max and Livia, had chosen to go out of state for college. After graduation, Emma had taken the inheritance from her maternal grandmother and used it to buy the building that now housed Wallflowers.

Wallflowers was a business that catered to people who enjoyed hand-crafted, artisan-made pieces. Emma loved it. Their eccentric store carried hand-carved cuckoo clocks, paintings, old-fashioned mirrors, masks, plaques...anything that could be used to decorate a wall. Becky had come up with the idea for the business and talked Emma into it over a long night of burritos and margaritas.

Emma paused to look around their "parlor". An antique rug covered the distressed hardwood floors. A small Victorian sofa covered in soft cream brocade graced the center of the floor. A Queen Anne coffee table in rich cherry wood sat before it, a silver tea service placed on it. Two Victorian chairs in that same cream fabric faced the sofa, creating a cozy little conversation group that the two women, and the occasional customer, used frequently. Against one wall was a gas fireplace with an ornately carved mantelpiece. On that mantelpiece were silver-framed photos, all of them either black and white or sepia toned. In one, Emma was dressed in a Victorian dress of ivory lace, a black cameo at her throat, her hair done up, a sweet smile on her face. In the other, Becky was dressed as a Wild West saloon girl, her frizzy hair teased out and feathers stuck in every which way. Her dress was pulled up on one side to show black boots and striped stockings. Neither photo had a place of prominence, both intermingled with other pictures. Unless you stood and went through the pictures thoroughly, you'd never find them.

A cherry and glass counter, as Victorian as they could make it and still have it be functional, graced one wall. On it sat an old-fashioned-looking cash register; hidden underneath the counter was the credit card reader.

They'd done their best to have the atmosphere of a bygone era and still keep the place warm and inviting. A fire crackled merrily in the fireplace on this cool October evening; the walls had a lovely cherry wood wainscoting, with rich rose floral wallpaper above it. It was very feminine, and both women loved it.

They'd had the store now for three years, and while they knew they'd never be rich off it, they also knew they'd never been happier.

Emma sighed, a smile of satisfaction on her face as she finished polishing the old, gilt-edged mirror they'd hung just behind the counter.

Life was good.

Dr. Max Cannon's life sucked. Once again he crossed the street, determined to avoid Livia's obvious attempt to get his attention. He'd been back in his small hometown for three months now, but she just couldn't get it through her overly highlighted head that he just wasn't interested. Hell, the woman's vision was perfect and yet she'd tried to schedule three different eye exams in the last three months! Thank God his partner Adrian was willing to run interference, or Max might have been forced to some extreme measures. Until he had a Curana who could safely deal with the woman, Livia was going to continue to be a serious problem. He ducked into the workshop of his best buddy and Beta, Simon Holt, determined to get away from the blonde barracuda bearing down on him.

"Hey, Max."

"Simon."

Simon's deferential nod was all that it should be from his Beta. "Hiding out from Livia again?"

The laughter in Simon's voice nearly had Max growling. "She's getting persistent."

"Have you told her to fuck off yet?"

Simon's approach to the pushy female was beginning to

appeal. The idea of her as his mate made his skin crawl. The Puma inside him yowled in protest. There was no way in hell he'd make her his Curana.

"No, but I'm getting there."

Simon pointed discreetly towards the workshop's front window. "Incoming."

Max gritted his teeth just as the door opened.

"Max, how nice to run into you!"

Soft, perfumed arms tried to circle his neck. In a swift move, Max glided away, turning to face the woman who'd tormented him since his return to Halle. "Livia."

It wasn't a greeting; it was a warning. Her eyes flared briefly with fear before she laughed it off. "I just wanted to remind you about the masquerade party over at Marie's. You'll be going, won't you?"

"Yes."

Livia frowned, her expression turning hard and calculating. "Most of the Pride will be there."

Max nodded; as Alpha he was well aware of that. Marie's father, the old Alpha, still held the annual masquerade at his house just outside of town. It was his pride and joy, that house, and he loved to entertain. His daughter, safely mated to Jamie Howard, acted as his hostess since the death of his mate some four years ago. Human and Puma mingled at the masquerade, the humans totally unaware of the Pumas in their midst. The Pride did its best to make the event a night to remember, for both races, and Jonathon Friedelinde did an excellent job of that. It was also the event at which an unmated male could unofficially signal his interest in a female. Hence Livia's interest in his attendance; if she could get him alone long enough, get him to signal in some way that there was a spark of interest, she could force him into a declaration he didn't want to make.

"Who are you taking?"

The question was asked with a seductive coyness that nearly made Max shudder. He suppressed it; he couldn't afford a sign of weakness. "At present, no one."

The chill in his voice should have made her back off. Instead, the stupid woman took it as a challenge. "Oh?" Her lashes fluttering coyly, she reached out with one manicured finger. When her blood red claw touched his chest, Max snarled a warning, his eyes flashing gold as the Puma warned her off.

With a gasp she backed away. Her head dipped in submission, an instinctive response to the Alpha power Max now exuded. It surrounded him in an unseen cloud, forcing all before him to do his will. Max rarely found himself in need of it, but today she'd pushed too far. She slowly backed away from him as a growl rumbled in his chest. He kept it going until she was completely out of Simon's workshop, pissed beyond belief at her persistence.

"Okay, I gotta admit, that was probably more effective than 'Fuck off, you skanky ho'. Think she got the message?"

And that was why Simon was his Beta—he'd flinched but stood his ground, something none of the other Pumas could do. Their reactions were more akin to Livia's when he chose to exercise his power.

He was also one of the few people Max trusted completely. If anything were to happen to Max, Simon would become Alpha.

Max turned with a laughing snort to answer his buddy's question when Simon's phone rang. His Beta punched the speakerphone button, still grinning at Max. "Hello?"

"Simon?" The voice on the other end of the phone drawled Simon's name with an amused authority that had Max's eyebrows rising into his hairline. He waited for Simon to put the woman in her place.

Simon rolled his eyes. "Hey, Emma."

Max blinked. Emma? Emma Carter?

"Your stained glass Madonna is late. Reverend Glaston is getting antsy."

Max blinked again. That sexy voice was *Emma*?

"I've been...distracted." That last was said with a quick glance at Max. He'd been the one keeping Simon busy. As Beta, Simon took care of a great deal of Pride business, something Emma wouldn't know about.

"Well, could you please ask your *distraction* to go home so you can finish the reverend's window?"

Her tone of voice raised Max's brows back into his hairline. His Beta's reaction had his jaw nearly dropping open.

"Emma," Simon nearly whined, "I've been working night and day, here. Give me a break!"

Emma?!? Plump little wallflower Emma?

"Just who have you been working, Simon Holt?"

Emma, who couldn't look him in the eye, making double entendres?

"No one, damn it! I've been working on...other things." Again, Simon shot Max a quick, furtive look.

Emma? *Emma* had his Beta shaking in his sneakers?

"Well, get your *thing* back under control and finish the reverend's window, okay?"

The irreverent authority in her voice stirred his interest. A vision of a dark-haired girl in a sunset-colored prom gown flashed through his mind.

"Damn it, Emma!" Simon sighed, leaning back against his workbench. "Where's Becky?"

The entreaty in Simon's voice barely registered. Max was

waiting to hear Emma's voice again.

"Oh, no, don't think you can get out of having that window finished today by sweet-talking Becky. I'm on to your tricks, buster."

Simon winced. Max's cock twitched.

Emma?

Hmmm. *Emma.*

"Okay, okay. I'll have the damn window done today. Anything else, Little General?" Simon's shoulders were quaking with laughter, his voice filled with respect. Max frowned at the affection in his Beta's voice.

"Mm-hmm. Becky and I will be going to the masquerade. Just thought you'd like to know."

Emma would be at the masquerade? Suddenly he was dying to see her. How had she turned out? Was she as sexy as her voice implied?

"Oh, yeah." The purr in Simon's voice had Max frowning. The small, predatory smile had his eyes flashing gold in protest as a wave of possessiveness rose inside him. The owner of that voice was *his.*

"Mm-hmm. See you later? *With* the window?"

"Count on it. Bye, Emma."

"Later, Simon."

Simon hung up the phone, that sexy smile still on his face. When he turned back, Max had himself back under control, merely raising a brow at Simon.

Simon flushed. "What?"

"When are you delivering that window?"

Simon looked over at the window waiting for its finishing touches. "Probably just after lunch. Why?"

"I'm going with you." Max grinned.

Simon straightened up, frowning slightly in confusion. "Why? I thought you had some other things to deal with."

"I want to check something out." At Simon's raised brow, Max's grin widened.

"Man, I'm not sure you want to go there."

Max's grin faded. "Why not?"

"Because Wallflowers has been known to suck the testosterone out of every single male who's ever entered."

"Huh?"

"It's pink. And frou-frou. And lacy. And *pink*."

Max laughed as Simon shuddered. "If your masculinity can handle it, so can mine."

Max watched his friend work on the stained glass window, his mind once again turning to Emma.

He hadn't seen her in eight years. She'd been seventeen, just about ready to graduate, smiling and laughing at the prom in a way he'd rarely seen her do. She'd been striking in her dress, a one-of-a-kind done in the colors of a rich autumn sunset, a strapless number in reds and golds with a sweetheart neckline and flaring skirt. He'd had a hard time keeping his eyes off her, but he'd been with Livia, and Max was not a man who cheated. By the time he'd broken up with Livia it was time for him to leave once again for college. Between earning his doctorate in optometry, his internship and residency, and learning from Jonathon how to run the Pride during his summers off, Emma had been quickly forgotten. Going out of state for college had been the right choice for him, and he'd been lucky that Jonathon agreed with him. Now, with his partnership with Adrian and Jonathon's official retirement he could finally start looking for his Curana. And he had a feeling he knew just who he wanted for the position.

She'd been sweetly innocent back then; slightly overweight, but with serious curves. It had been that innocence, and Livia, that had held him back.

She didn't sound so innocent now, and Livia was nowhere in the picture.

It was definitely time he got better acquainted with little Miss Emma.

Emma watched as Simon's shiny red pickup truck pulled up to the curb of Wallflowers. She grinned, knowing Becky had hidden in the back office to avoid meeting up with Simon. Simon was the only person on the face of the planet who made Becky lose the power of speech. In an odd, karmic sort of way, Emma had no problem handling the hunky Simon, laughing and chatting with him with ease.

Emma watched Simon climb out of the truck. The passenger side opened up as well, and a familiar tall blond got out, a grin on his face, his unbound hair blown about by the cool autumn breeze.

Emma was horrified. *Oh, no. Not* him! She took a deep breath to steady her nerves. She was no longer the shy teenager he'd once known; she was a grown woman with a shop of her own. She could handle Max Cannon.

Then he grinned at something Simon said, and her hands began to shake. She took another quick breath and blew it out, trying desperately to steady her racing heart.

The two men wrestled the stained glass window out of the flatbed of the truck. With care, they got it to the door of the shop. Emma rushed to open it just as the reverend arrived.

Reverend Glaston smiled at the two men. "Hello, Simon,

Max. Is that the church's window?"

Emma smiled at the reverend. He was a kind soul, with smiling whisky brown eyes and balding gray hair. He never failed to make Emma feel comfortable, and she was counting on that now to get her through *his* presence.

"Sure is, Reverend. Let's get it inside so I can show it to you."

Simon's deep voice reverberated through her, making her shiver a little. If she weren't so hung up on the blond hunk behind him, she'd have made a play for Simon a long time ago. Although, considering how Becky had always reacted to him...

"Becky? Can you come give me a hand with this?" Emma yelled into the back, struggling to hide her grin when Simon's gaze glued itself to the curtained-off area that led to their office. *Okay, maybe I wouldn't have gone after Simon.*

She heard Becky's muttered oath as she stomped into the front room. Simon's gaze never left Becky as he and Max maneuvered the window into the store. His dark brown eyes heated as Becky scowled at him and took a step back.

"Becky?" Emma asked, waving her forward. With a false cheerfulness, Becky smiled at Emma, then joined her by the propped-up window.

"Emma?" Emma turned to Simon, who was staring at her now. "You remember Max, right?"

He's kinda hard to forget, Emma thought as Max stepped forward.

"Hi, Emma."

She looked up, getting a quick peek at the face that had starred in every single one of her naughty fantasies before lowering them to the scar next to his nose. "Hi, Max."

He cleared his throat, a sound filled with amusement. She

glanced back up at him to see him staring at her with a raised brow. Looking down, she noticed he'd held out his hand. With a false smile she took it, pumping it up and down twice before dropping it like a hot potato.

Her heart fluttering from just that simple touch, she turned to Simon, the lesser of the two threats. "So, Simon, are you ready to unveil your masterpiece?" Her smile for him was genuine; she truly liked Simon. His work was exquisite. On top of that, he had one of the best senses of humor she'd ever seen. It felt like having a brother, something she'd never had the pleasure of experiencing, being an only child.

He lifted one brow, grinning at her. "Yes, Little General. Right away, Little General."

Putting her hands on her hips, she glared at him. Although, from the twitching of his lips, he wasn't all that impressed. "*Now*, Simon."

She could hear the reverend coughing on a laugh behind her. Simon just rolled his eyes and began unwrapping the window.

When it was finally unveiled, Emma was astonished. It was easily one of Simon's finest works. The Madonna sat, her blue robes gently waving around her, a small Mona Lisa smile on her face as she stared down at the dark-haired baby held gently in her arms. The Madonna was beautiful, but it wasn't a classic beauty. It was the gentleness in her face, the love she so obviously bore her child that made it so special. He'd managed to capture that special smile that new mothers everywhere gave their newborns, and it took an otherwise normal face and made it radiant.

"My God, Simon. It's gorgeous," Max breathed from right behind her.

"Thanks." Simon's eyes didn't rest on the Madonna,

though; they were on Becky, who stared at the Madonna with something akin to awe. "Becky?"

Becky's gaze went from the Madonna to him. The reverence on her face seemed to stun Simon, who drew in a quick breath.

Emma felt Max stir behind her. When one of his hands came to rest at her hip, she nearly jumped out of her skin. "Well!" She clapped her hands, moving away from the dangerous heat of the man behind her to go to the reverend. Not surprisingly, Becky, after nearly jumping out of her skin, refused to meet Simon's eyes again.

"What do you think, Reverend?" She put on her best salesman's voice, for once not flustered to be using it in front of real people.

The reverend's slow smile was all the answer she needed.

Hot damn, Max thought, watching the little dynamo that was Emma in action. *Why the hell didn't I stop here sooner?* He'd been busy setting up his practice, true, but you'd think he'd have made the time to stop by. Be neighborly.

When Max had stepped out of the truck, he hadn't really been expecting much; after all, most women couldn't live up to the voice Emma had. It was slightly husky, like she'd spent the night moaning in some man's arms, a visual Max could do without. She managed to infuse it with an authority that had his Beta jumping to do her bidding, something that spoke to the Puma in him. Max wondered if she'd try to take the lead in bed, as well. A challenge, that; he loved taking a strong woman and reducing her to a quivering, begging mass of bliss.

Her straight, dark brown hair was caught up in a ponytail that hung to just between her shoulder blades. Big brown eyes dominated her face, artfully made up to accentuate them. Her lips were slicked with a pale rose. Her features weren't classically beautiful, but something about the animation in them drew Max like nothing else ever had.

And her body...

Hell, her *body...*

The top of her head barely reached his shoulder, something he normally wasn't attracted to, but on Emma it aroused protective instincts he didn't even know he possessed. She had the most sweetly rounded ass encased in tight black jeans and the most magnificent breasts Max had ever been privileged to watch bounce under a lacy rose camisole. With a real waist and hips a man could grab on to for the ride of his life, she reminded him of an old-fashioned pin-up girl, all soft curves and feminine strength. Then she turned, laughing up at something Simon said, sensuous and innocent at the same time, and Max was a goner.

Holy. Fucking. Damn.

Emma. Little Emma Carter sure as hell had grown up.

His hands burned to touch her again. That fleeting touch she'd allowed him had merely whetted his appetite. He longed to rip that camisole off her body and feast at her breasts, hear her moans as he slipped her jeans down those incredible, edible legs, her soft cries as he feasted on her juices.

She would scream his name as she came.

He would tie her to his bed, torture her into ecstasy, and then start all over again. He'd bend her over the arm of his couch and take her from behind over and over until she begged him to come, biting into her shoulder and marking her as his for all to see. The thought of slipping his cock into that luscious ass nearly made him come right there in the middle of her store.

When she laughingly hugged Simon, he nearly went for his Beta's throat.

Mine!

Only Simon saw the way his eyes gleamed gold, heard the low, purring growl that erupted from his throat before he could stop himself. Sucking in a breath, Max turned away, desperately trying to get himself under control.

He'd been told he'd know his mate when he met her; now he knew what they meant. He'd spoken to Emma when she'd been a teenager, felt a little spark of *something*, but had dismissed it as nothing serious. Just young lust. Now he knew what that spark had been and wanted to kick his own ass. Not all Pumas got lucky enough to find his or her mate; to know he'd not only met her, but walked away from her, hell, *forgotten* her, galled him.

He forced himself to look around her shop, at anything but the laughing group of people around the Madonna, before he walked over there, plucked her up and carted her out of her shop to somewhere private.

She'd done well for herself. Emma's stamp, mixed with Becky's, created an atmosphere both women seemed at home in. He could see women flocking to the store, much to the horror and amusement of their male companions. He walked over to the mantelpiece, seeing a silver picture frame his mother would probably appreciate as a gift for her birthday. Something about the picture in it drew his attention. He leaned forward, trying to see why the Victorian lady in it looked so familiar when he felt a small hand touch his arm.

"Is everything okay between you and Simon?"

That husky voice, combined with her soft touch, had his cock once more threatening to burst out of his jeans. He looked down into her face and saw nothing there but concern. Before she could move, he put his hand over hers, trapping her at his side. He was ridiculously pleased when she didn't try to pull away. "Everything is fine between me and Simon." *As long as he keeps his paws off of you.*

She looked away, back towards the group, and bit her lip. "Can I talk to you for a moment?"

Her voice was hesitant, shy in a way she wasn't when she talked to Simon or the reverend, but her expression begged him to say yes. A fierce wave of protectiveness rose in him, and his hand tightened over hers. He nodded.

He allowed her to pull them to the side, quiet and private but still in plain view. She looked up at him again, obviously uncertain before she focused, damn it, back on his scar. "Um, do you have any idea how Simon feels about Becky?"

She peeked up at him again before dropping her gaze once more. A flush rose in her cheeks and she bit her lip again.

He took a deep breath, striving to control the possessiveness that roared through him. "Not a clue."

Her softly muttered "damn" had him nearly smiling, it was so filled with aggravation, but the possessive monster in him couldn't get past her possible interest in his best friend. "He's not for you." He could feel wisps of his power flowing out of his control, trying to force her to acknowledge the truth of his words.

Emma looked him full in the face for the first time since he'd entered the store. He knew he sounded like a caveman, and probably looked like a jealous jackass, but he couldn't help it; little Emma did that to him.

Then she laughed at him. Not one bit intimidated, frightened or cowed.

"Not me, you idiot." His eyes widened in astonishment as she turned back to the group around the Madonna. "Becky. She's had a thing for him since high school, but she can't seem to act on it and he's never shown any real interest." She looked back up at him. “Until recently, that is. So, I wanted to know, you being his best friend, if you know how he feels.”

He felt his whole body tense at the devilish calculation on her face. “What are you planning?” He maneuvered his body, and hers, until they were in the corner, effectively cutting her off from the crowd behind them. His power was back under control, but his curiosity was roused.

She puffed out an impatient breath, focusing once more on him. Some of her shyness had evaporated, but in its place was an irritation he wasn’t used to seeing in feminine eyes. “Becks and I are going to the annual masquerade. Mr. Friedelinde invited us, for the first time. I’m hoping I can get either Simon or Becky moving in the right direction, but I don’t want Becky hurt or embarrassed if Simon isn’t really interested.” She looked up at him, her little chin tilted as she demanded a response. “So. Is he?”

Max turned back to look at his Beta. From the way Simon was sniffing the air around Becky, he’d say Simon was *very* interested. He looked down at Emma, who was tapping her foot impatiently. “Yes.”

Relief flickered across her face and her body relaxed as if he’d lifted a weight off her shoulders. “Thank God. They’d be perfect together.”

“What makes you say that?” Truly curious, he watched as she turned thoughtful.

“Simon knows he can have any female he wants just by snapping his fingers, but Becky backs away from him every time he approaches. He’s never quite certain where he stands with her. He gets bored so easily with the ones that fall in the palm of his hand that he winds up dumping them pretty quickly. He can’t predict what Becky will do, so she’d never bore him. Also, Becky loves his work and understands how much time and devotion it takes to make the kinds of things Simon does, so she wouldn't resent that if she knew he'd be coming home to her. She would challenge him; keep him on his toes, while he would cherish her like she should be cherished. No one's truly loved her before, or shown her her own worth." Emma focused on him again, her expression gleefully vengeful. "But if he hurts her, I'll scoop out his nuts with a grapefruit spoon."

The change from dreamer to avenger had Max grinning even as his balls drew up at the visual image she'd created; although, from the way Simon was acting she had nothing to worry about. "Remind me not to get you mad at me."

"Oh, no, I'm not the one to be afraid of." She motioned him closer with a crooked finger, and he obligingly bent closer, getting a whiff of her rose-scented perfume as he did. "Becky had a friend in college who showed her how to use a goat emasculator," she whispered softly in his ear.

Max reared back, staring at Becky and then back down to the innocent-looking little devil nodding solemnly in front of him.

He threw his head back and laughed harder than he had in months.

Max climbed into Simon's truck with a grin.

"What the hell did Emma say to you to get you to laugh like that, anyway?" Simon asked, his tone aggravated.

Max shook his head. "Nothing you'd be interested in, I'm sure."

"Try me," Simon snarled.

Max snarled a warning to his Beta, who had the grace to look guilty.

"Sorry."

"Want to tell me what that was all about?"

Max wasn't asking, and Simon knew that. He sighed. "Becky. She won't talk to me, barely looks at me and leaves the room the minute I enter it. Hell, if she can arrange it she makes sure she's gone before I get there!"

"So you're not interested in Emma?"

The look Simon shot him was part amazement, part horror, and Max relaxed, his fears that Simon was interested in Emma eased. It was the look a brother would give someone if asked if he thought his sister was hot.

"Emma wants to do something to bring the two of you together. I thought I'd verify that it's what you want before I start helping her."

"Man, if you and Emma can get Becky to agree to give me a chance, I'd be forever grateful." Simon shook his head, frowning ferociously. "I have no idea what I did to turn her off me so thoroughly, but if something doesn't give soon I'm going to lose it." Simon looked thoroughly miserable. "I'm pretty sure she's my mate."

Max mentally rubbed his hands together in anticipation. "We'll see what we can do."

He ignored Simon's sideways glance, his Beta's slow grin too close to a smirk. "Emma sure grew up pretty, didn't she?"

Max tried his best, but he couldn't hold back his grin. "Yes, she did."

Simon nodded his approval. "She'd make a great Curana."

Max smiled. The idea of Emma as his Curana, ruling at his side, mated to him for all eternity appealed mightily. Not one to waste time when he wanted something, he began outlining his plan to win over their women.

Chapter Two

Emma turned the sign over to "Closed", pulled down the shade and locked the door, sighing in happy exhaustion.

The reverend had *loved* Simon's Madonna. She wondered if she was the only one who'd noticed the Madonna looked something like Becky. It had been the only thing that had given her the courage to approach Max; that and the look on Becky's face when she'd stared at Simon. Of course, the way Simon had followed Becky's every move hadn't hurt, either.

Max had been surprisingly easy to talk to, once she got over her initial shyness. His nearness had sent her heart pounding, tying her tongue in knots, as usual, until his ridiculous announcement that Simon wasn't for her.

Duh. Simon was for Becky.

She pulled the creamy, lacy shade down over the big picture window, effectively closing her in the twilight gloom of the shop. Becky had already rung out the register and was happily doing the accounts in the back, a pot of coffee and a huge container of Kung Pao chicken at her elbow while Emma finished closing down the front.

Emma loved this time of the evening. The streets were quiet, except for a few people heading either home or to their favorite restaurant for dinner. The soft light of early evening cast a glow over everything it touched, making it seem softer, more romantic. With a sigh, Emma headed into the back to gather up her coat and purse. With a wave to Becky, who waved her fork back with a grin, Emma slipped out of the back of the store.

"Emma."

Emma shrieked, staggering back and pulling her can of mace out of her pocket before realizing that the man standing in the shadows was Max. "God damn it, Max!"

"Sorry." He didn't sound all that sorry; he sounded like he was trying not to laugh. "Don't break out the grapefruit spoon just yet."

Her heart was still beating a mile a minute. She put the mace away and glared at him. "What?"

"Well, jeez, is that any way to greet someone who's here to help you?"

Putting her hand to her chest, Emma glared at him in the dim light. The son of a bitch *was* laughing at her. "Help me with what?"

"Getting Becky and Simon together, of course."

"Huh?" He looked entirely too smug as he moved closer to her.

"You want to get Simon and Becky together? I can help you with that." He picked up her arm and placed it through his, trapping her hand beneath his own. Suddenly he frowned and looked around. "Where is Becky, by the way?"

"She's still inside, working on the accounts," she answered absently, momentarily distracted by the feel of his arm under her own. It felt like it was hewn from rock, strong and solid and probably immovable.

His face blanked. "You came out here, at night, by yourself." It wasn't a question, it was a statement. He sounded like he couldn't quite believe his ears.

"Yeah. I do that every night. I'm parked right over there." She pointed with her free hand and gently tried to extract her other one from his suddenly iron grip. Becky lived in the apartment over the shop while Emma lived in an apartment in a complex on the other side of town. When Becky was done with the accounts, and her Chinese, she'd probably head upstairs to her tiny apartment and veg in front of her TV.

"You carry mace. I assume that means there's some crime in this area."

She nodded slowly. "There's crime everywhere, even here, what with the college nearby."

He was beginning to worry her. His face was still blank, but something about his eyes had changed. They glittered strangely, almost as if he were angry. She decided not to tell him why she carried the mace.

"Have you been attacked out here before?"

Emma winced and quickly tried to cover up the telltale sign by babbling. "It's perfectly safe out here, and Becky keeps an ear out for the sound of my car. Any minute now she's going to run out here ready to annihilate anyone who's bothering me, so you might wanna let up on the death grip!" Her wince was now one of pain as his hand squeezed hers in a vise-like grip.

He let go and stared down at her. She could have sworn his eyes were gold in the moonlight before he blinked, the illusion fading back into his normal blue as he prowled around her, circling her like a predator. "Who hurt you, Emma?"

"What is wrong with you?" Emma took back her hand and rubbed it, wondering if she'd have a bruise. She glared up at him, waiting for an answer.

Max's frown was fierce. "I want to know who hurt you, Emma. I want to know now."

The note of command in his voice was one she'd never heard from anyone before. He compelled her to answer him in a primal way, forcing her body back against the brick wall of the shop with his own, looming over her in a way that both frightened and soothed her. Part of her wanted to bow down submissively and answer anything he asked of her. It took every ounce of her will to sniff and reply, "I have no idea what you're talking about."

She saw the shock on his face as she turned her head away, dismissing him. She ducked under his arm and started walking towards her car, her back stiff, her chin high. "You know, not every woman appreciates the caveman routine. Why don't you try it out on Livia? I'm sure she'd appreciate it!"

She gasped as her body was yanked back into the hardness of his. She could feel him in every atom, as if he was deliberately imprinting himself there. "If I'm reacting this way, how do you think Simon will react when he hears Becky's here alone?"

Emma gulped. *Becky who?* Involuntarily her hand came up and grasped the arm around her waist, her nails digging in with pleasure at the strength in it.

"Um, I don't know?" God, her brains were completely scrambled if that was the best she could do. "Hit her over the head with a club and drag her off by her hair? Not that he'd have all that far to go; she lives over the store, for God's sake."

He leaned down, his lips tickling her ear, his hair brushing hers, blending with hers. His other arm came around her waist, pulling her tighter into his body. She felt completely surrounded. She could feel his erection against her lower back, hot and hard as an iron bar, and gulped. "Why do you carry mace, Emma?"

"Why do you care, Max?" She tried to ignore the feel of his

lips as he—

Did he just kiss my ear?

"Emma. Tell me what I want to know."

"And you'll go away?" She tried to ignore the incredible feeling of him gently rocking her in his arms. *Yeah. That's it, I'm gonna start struggling any minute now. Any minute...*

"Hell, no." He laughed gruffly. He put his chin on the top of her head and continued to rock her. When her stomach rumbled embarrassingly beneath his hands, he stilled. "Emma? Am I keeping you from your dinner?"

"At this point, you're keeping me from my dinner AND late night snack."

"Hmmm. In that case, I suggest we go out to eat. Maybe after I feed you you'll be more willing to tell me what I want to know." He sounded positively cheerful as he grabbed her hand, whirled her around and half dragged her towards his blue Durango.

"Gee, Captain Caveman, care to slow down? I didn't agree to go out to dinner with you."

He huffed out another laugh and opened the SUV's door. "In you go!" He gently lifted her into the seat. "Food. Then fight. Okay?" And with a smile he pushed her legs inside the SUV and shut the door.

She considered opening the door and hopping out, but part of her (okay, the majority of her) wanted to see what the hell Max was up to. Plus, hello! Dinner with Max! Could there be a downside to this?

She snapped on her seat belt as he got into the car. She hadn't enjoyed sparring with someone this much for a long time. "Don't think you're going to get what you want just because you buy me dinner."

"I wouldn't dream of it," Max purred, starting the SUV.

"Oh, boy," Emma muttered as Max, with another choked off laugh, drove out of the parking lot.

Max pulled the SUV up to his favorite restaurant, Noah's. He slid out, fully intending to open Emma's door and assist her down but she beat him to it, hopping out of the cab of his SUV with ease.

"Didn't your mother ever teach you to let the man open your door for you?" he asked, amused, as he followed her to the doors of the restaurant.

She rolled her eyes at him over her shoulder. "It's not like this is a date, Max." She flipped her ponytail back over her shoulder with a defiant flick of her wrist. "It's more like a kidnapping. With food."

He had to press his lips together to keep from laughing out loud. "Do you want my help with Simon and Becky, or not?"

"At the rate they're going we'll be ninety before they get together, so, yeah, anything that will help speed that up would be good."

He managed to reach the door before she did, opening it up and placing a hand at the small of her back as she sailed through. He kept that hand there, reveling in the feel of her strong, sleek back as he maneuvered her towards the hostess.

"Max! Wonderful to see you."

Max smiled what he called his social smile at Belinda Campbell, hostess at Noah's. He ignored her curious stare with ease, all of his attention focused on the woman beneath his hand.

"Table for two, Belinda."

"Coming right up, Max." Her full red lips curled up with a

hint of contempt. “Business dinner, Max?”

Max looked up at Belinda through his lashes, his eyes flashing briefly gold in warning. “Pleasure.”

Just as Emma said, “Business.”

Max turned his attention back to Emma, noted the way her chin was tilted, and grinned. She was still pissed off about being “kidnapped”. “Perhaps both.”

Belinda’s brows rose in disbelief as she gathered their menus. “Right this way.”

As she sashayed across the restaurant to Max’s preferred table, Emma whispered, “Gee, I get the feeling she doesn’t like me.”

“I wouldn’t worry about whether or not Belinda likes you,” Max whispered back as he helped her out of her light jacket and assisted her into her chair. Bending over, he whispered into her ear, delighted when she shivered. “Worry about whether or not *I* like you.”

He sat himself across from her, enjoying the flush high on her cheekbones. When she cleared her throat and snapped open the menu between them, he nearly growled in frustration. Watching her face, her expressions, the way her eyes lit up or went dreamy, was becoming an obsession.

The more time he spent with her, the more she fascinated him. She amused him with her wit, aroused him with a glance, frustrated him with her avoidance, and forced him to deal with her in a way very few people could. When he’d used his power to force an answer out of her in that alley, she’d actually walked away from him, back turned, head held high.

He still couldn’t decide if he wanted to fuck her or spank her for that.

If he played his cards right, he’d get to do both.

"So, the seafood alfredo is supposed to be really good here," Emma croaked, her eyes glued to the dinner choices on the page in front of her rather than the dinner of choice sitting across from her.

After a brief hesitation, Max answered, his tone light and easy. "I'm more of a traditionalist myself. I think I'll go with the manicotti." He put his menu down, then gently pried hers out of her hands. "Salad or soup?"

"Um, salad, I think."

Max nodded with satisfaction. When the waiter appeared, he quickly placed their orders, going with wine to drink, chardonnay for her and merlot for himself.

She crossed her arms and glared at him. "What if I wanted something else to drink?"

"I thought, with your scare in the alley, you wouldn't mind something to help you wind down." He smiled, sensuous and predatory, nearly causing her to fall off her chair. "Relax, Emma. Enjoy the moment."

Without thinking, she blurted out the first thing that popped into her head. "Are you flirting with me?"

He blinked, then laughed, low and soft, taking her hand in his and gently stroking her palm with his thumb. She could feel the sensation of his fingers all the way down to her womb. "What do you think?"

"I think I'll need more wine," she deadpanned, completely flabbergasted.

Max Cannon was flirting. With *her*.

When Max chuckled, she tried prying her hand out of his, with no luck. Deciding to completely ignore his heated stare, she tried switching topics. "So, how do you plan on helping me with Simon and Becky?" She raised her brows in silent command, demanding he answer her while trying to hide the fact that her insides were melting into a puddle of aroused goo.

He leaned back with a sigh. "Actually, I was hoping you had a plan and I could just lend a hand."

"I know Simon is going to the masquerade on Saturday night; do you know what costume he plans on wearing?"

Max frowned at her, thinking. "Technically, the costumes are supposed to be a secret."

"You're going as Zorro."

"Where did you hear that?"

"Livia and Marie were gossiping in the grocery store while I was there." Emma grimaced, remembering how Livia had treated her that day, with a mixture of false pity and contempt. Livia and Belinda were best friends, which meant that Livia would shortly hear of her little "business" dinner with Max, which meant Livia would be confronting her sometime in the near future. Emma sighed; dealing with Livia in a snit was never a fun time.

He shook his head. "Listening to gossip, Emma?"

His face was mockingly sad, the hint of laughter finally clueing her in. She could practically hear the little light bulb go off over her head. "Let me guess. *Simon* is Zorro."

"Got it in one."

"Wow. Livia's going to be disappointed." Emma tried to control her giggle, but it slipped out anyway.

"I think I can live with Livia's disappointment." Cradling his glass in one hand, her hand still firmly clasped in his other, Max took a sip of his wine, looking extremely pleased with himself. "Let me guess, she immediately bought a Spanish senorita?"

"Complete with Spanish comb, mantilla and fan."

Max confined himself to shaking his head as the waiter arrived with their food. After the waiter left, he let go of her hand so they could both eat. "So, what are you going as?"

His tone was casual, but his look was anything but. "I'm not sure. Becky and I haven't had a chance to go shopping yet."

Max's fork paused. He looked at her, his face filled with unholy amusement. "I have an idea."

Emma raised her brows in enquiry as she licked a bit of alfredo sauce off of her fork. "What idea?"

Max gazed at her mouth, his eyes darkening with obvious desire. "Hmm?"

Emma snapped her fingers at him. "What idea?"

He looked up, the heat in his gaze nearly scorching her. "I have several ideas," he purred. "Which would you like to hear first?"

Emma opened her mouth, but nothing came out. With a startled snap, she shut it, turning her attention once again to her dinner to avoid the satisfied male smirk across the table.

After a few minutes of silence, Emma felt like she once again had the power of speech. "So, what's your idea?" When he looked at her like he wanted to devour her, Emma quickly clarified, "For the masquerade!"

"Becky goes as a female Zorro. If Becky's uncomfortable with that, we can have Simon change his costume so the two of them match."

Emma sat back in her chair, frowning in thought. "Becky's been talking about doing a lady pirate—"

"No."

Emma blinked slowly, unsure whether or not to be pissed or amused at the firm order. "Okay," she drawled, "and your suggestion would be?"

"How about a saloon girl?"

Emma choked on her wine. "Um, saloon girl?"

"Yes. Simon can dress as a cowboy. Is there a problem with that?"

Emma bit her lip. "Maybe." She latched onto the first thing she could think of to change his mind; Becky would *never* wear the saloon girl outfit in public! She kept the picture of herself in that outfit all the way in the back on the mantelpiece. "Becky's self-conscious about her lack of...attributes."

Max looked confused. "Attributes?"

Emma could feel herself turning red. "Boobies," she hissed, looking around to see if anyone heard her.

Max choked. "She's worried about her breast size?"

Emma nodded, shushing him with her hand.

Max sighed. "Okay, how about a flapper? Simon can pull off a gangster look, I think."

Emma thought about dark, dangerous-looking Simon and nodded. Suddenly she flapped her hands at him in excitement as she remembered a costume she'd seen online. "Oh! What about a fallen angel? I saw this really sexy number that would look incredible on Becky!"

"Have you ever looked at men's devil costumes? They're cheesy." Max frowned in thought. "No, we need something they'll both be comfortable in."

Emma grinned. "I saw bat wings he could wear over his shoulders. Put him in a trench coat with the wings, leather pants, bare-chested..." Emma waved a hand in front of her face, making Max scowl. "Believe me, women will pass out from the heat."

Max picked up her hand and stared into her eyes. "Really?"

he asked softly. With careless elegance, he took her hand to his mouth, gently nibbling the back of her knuckles.

Once again Emma felt her cheeks heat. “Stop that!” She snatched her hand back and put it in her lap for safe-keeping. She cleared her throat and willed herself back into the costume conversation. “Becky has a romantic streak a mile wide. Maybe we can work with that.”

“Hmm. How about Robin Hood and Maid Marian?”

“Done to death.”

“Which leaves out paired vampires?”

“Yup. You know, maybe Lady Zorro isn’t such a bad idea, after all. And even better, Becky knows a bit about fencing, so she’ll be comfortable wearing a sword.”

“She can use the sword on Simon if he doesn’t get the message?”

“Something like that.” Emma sat back with a sigh as the waiter appeared. Both decided on dessert, Emma going for the French silk pie and Max picking raspberry cheesecake. Max had coffee; Emma took another glass of wine.

“The only other thing Becky’s interested in is Trinity from the Matrix. Think Simon wants to be Neo?”

Max shook his head. “As alluring as Becky would be in a leather cat suit, I think Simon would prefer Zorro.”

“Okay. Then it’s settled. I’ll see about getting Becky’s costume.”

“Don’t worry about it. I’ll pick up Becky’s costume when I pick up your costume.”

Once again she was ready to throttle him. “And what costume will I be wearing?”

Max grinned. “It’s a surprise.”

“A surprise?”

Max picked up her hand and nibbled on her knuckles again, effectively shutting down her brain in the process. "Mm-hmm."

"Oh."

With a look of satisfaction, Max put her hand back down on the table. "Are you going to finish your dessert?"

Emma looked down at her pie, suddenly no longer hungry. She took a deep breath and asked the question she knew she was going to have to ask before they ever entered the restaurant. "How will I find you at the masquerade?" At his raised brow she added hastily, "If we're supposed to make sure Simon and Becky find each other, we need to make sure we can find each other too."

"Don't worry, it won't be a problem."

Max's purr sent a shiver through her. "Okay." Emma bit her lip, wondering if she should ask her next question. "Will your date mind you helping me out? I mean, I wouldn't want to make things awkward between you and your current girlfriend, whoever she is."

"Do you think I would ask you out to dinner if I was seeing someone, Emma?"

Emma raised her eyebrows, clearly amused. "Well, if you'd *asked* me..."

"*Emma.*"

"I mean, the food part of the kidnapping was kinda nice."

"Very well. Would I be trying to seduce you if I was seeing someone?"

Emma opened her mouth to make the comment that first sprang to her lips, but seeing the serious expression on his face she bit it back. Instead, she went with her second thought. "I don't know. You've been gone a long time. For all I know, you're gay."

It was Max's turn to open his mouth and have nothing come out.

Emma lifted her hand to the waiter. "Check, please."

"I'm not gay." Max stalked to the Durango, trying to decide if he was insulted or not.

Emma shrugged carelessly. "Bi then."

"Emma!"

He was forced to stop when she collapsed against the side of the car, giggling like a schoolgirl. The only thing she managed to gasp in between bouts of giggling was, "Oh, God, the look on your face!"

Max shook his head, wondering, knowing she had no idea how few people dared tease him. How the hell had he missed this woman all those years ago? He could have dated Emma back then instead of Livia. He'd have had Emma all these years, laughing at him, teasing him, driving him insane. The thought of his own blindness where she was concerned made him grit his teeth in frustration.

No more. Never again would he allow himself to do without Emma.

Crossing his arms, he leaned against the car door and waited for her to stop laughing. "You finished?" he asked indulgently, his heart beating a strange tattoo at the sound of her laughter.

She wiped the tears away with a final giggle. "Yeah, I think so."

"Good." With a swiftness only another Puma could match, Max snatched her close, bent down and kissed her. She barely had time to gasp.

That small gasp of surprise gave him immediate access to her mouth. He stroked inside her, slow and deep, just like he wanted to take her. He savored her taste, wine, chocolate and woman, and his head reeled. When her lips finally began to move against his, he moaned, his cock twitching like she was stroking him there with her wet heat. Her tongue dueled with his with a shyness that once again brought out his protective instincts. Without thought, he turned her so that her back rested against the Durango, his broad shoulders and back hiding her from the view of those in the restaurant.

No one but him would ever get to see her passion again.

He wanted to open the door, lay her down on the seat, and strip her naked. He wanted to be sheathed so far in her body she'd be able to taste him in the back of her throat. He wanted to mark her with his scent, his seed, and his teeth so badly he shook with it.

But they were on a public road, outside a very public restaurant; he couldn't do any of the things he wanted to do so badly, except...

With a snarl he lifted his mouth from hers and buried it against her throat.

"Max," she whispered in that soft, husky voice.

He suckled at the sensitive juncture of her throat and shoulder until she lay quiet and panting in his arms, her face buried in his shoulder. Gently he scraped the area with his teeth to prepare her. One hand slid down to cup her ass, reveling in the feel of her full curves; the other held her to him with a grip of iron, hard around her back. He had to concentrate not to dig his claws in and knead. He pushed between her legs with his knee until she was practically riding his thigh. With a rumbling purr he bit down, drawing blood and injecting her with the enzyme that would change her, marking her for all time as his. Her cry was muffled by his shirt; feeling her shivers he realized she was climaxing from the effect of the bite, riding his thigh as his essence and hers mingled.

He lapped at the small wound, not surprised to see it was already closing. With his mark on her and her orgasm, some of his own urgency left him. She was his.

Chapter Three

Emma was still reeling from whatever the hell it was Max had done to her with his bite when he gently helped her into the Durango. Her hands were shaking so badly she couldn't even put her seat belt on without help.

She'd never come so hard in all her life. And he hadn't even gotten her naked. She desperately tried to ignore the little voice that asked, *if it was that good upright and clothed, how would it feel with him naked and inside me?* She shivered.

"Are you okay?"

Emma tried to ignore the way her cheeks were heating, instead focusing on the purring amusement she could hear in his voice. "I'm fine," she squeaked. Clearing her throat, she tried again. "I, um..." Her voice trailed off as Max took her hand in his, placing it on his hard thigh. She had to clear her throat again, shaking her head violently to see if she could get her brain cells to start working again. "Ah, Saturday...when will you be picking up the costumes?"

Max smiled lazily. "I'll head to the costume shop tomorrow and get them, don't worry about it."

"When will you drop them off?"

Max was silent for a moment, obviously thinking. "Would Becky wear a costume from a secret admirer, or would it be better coming from you?"

Emma bit her lip, her attention once again focused on Becky's problem rather than the tall blond problem at her side. "I'm not sure. If I told her I'd gotten the costume, she might feel more comfortable about wearing it."

Max smiled. "We'll do that, then." His shoulders went back and his head tilted as he looked down at her briefly, the determination in his eyes completely wiping out the earlier humor. They seemed to gleam gold under a passing street lamp before he turned back to the road. "Now you're going to explain to me why you carry mace in your pocket." That odd note of command was back in his voice as he drove away from Noah's, demanding a reply.

Emma shrugged and ignored the urge to put her head down. "No reason, I just think a woman alone should carry protection and I don't like the thought of guns."

"Don't lie to me, Emma."

Emma's chin tilted up. "I'm not lying." She sniffed. "I don't like guns."

"Emma," he growled.

"Oh, pooh, you don't scare me, so stop growling," she yawned. She turned to look at him. "Anyway, should Becky carry her own rapier or would it be better to have her carry a toy?"

Max's jaw was moving, like he was grinding his teeth. "I can find out. Would you rather tell me, or let me go looking?"

"Wow," Emma breathed. "I've heard of that, but never actually seen it."

He looked at her quizzically out of the corner of his eye. "Seen what?"

"You actually talked through clenched teeth. I didn't think

anyone really did that, you know?"

He pulled over and put the car out of gear. "Emma, why don't you want to tell me what happened?"

"Oh, gee, maybe because it's none of your business?"

His utter stillness surprised her; she wasn't even certain he breathed for a moment. When he turned his head with exaggerated slowness, she realized she'd finally succeeded in pissing him off. "Everything about you is my business, Emma."

She was shocked at his dangerous tone of voice. "Max?"

"You're mine, Emma, and I protect what's mine."

Her jaw dropped in disbelief. "*What?*"

He put the car back in gear, taking off with a squeal of tires. "You heard me."

"Uh, excuse me, but one kidnapping with food does not make Emma your property!"

"You bear my mark."

She blinked, totally confused. The feral light in his eyes hadn't lessened. The Durango was roaring as Mad Max drove like a bat out of hell for the outskirts of town. "What the hell are you talking about?"

"I bit you."

"And? You think you're the first guy to give me a hickey? *Shit!*" Emma made a grab for the door as Max took a turn at high speed.

"I don't think I need to hear about you and other men right now, Emma."

"Okay, okay! Could you slow down, please?"

Max looked away from the road long enough to see her glaring at him. With a rough sigh he slowed down. "Look, I know you're confused."

"No, I think you're the one who's confused. Have you forgotten to take your medication today? Is that it? You turn into psycho-boy while in college?"

Max ran an impatient hand through his hair. "This isn't the way I wanted to do this," he muttered gruffly.

"Look, I promise I'm not jealous that the voices only speak to you, okay?"

Max pulled off the main road and onto a side road, shaking his head. "Emma, we need to talk."

The tone of his voice made her sit back. He sounded...odd, like he knew whatever he had to tell her was something she wouldn't want to hear. "We talked. We talked all through dinner. Why are we out in the middle of nowhere to talk, by the way?"

He sighed. "Because there are certain things you may want to see that I can't show you in the middle of town."

"Uh-huh. I think your thing can go without being seen tonight."

The Durango jerked to a stop. There was a stunned silence for a moment. "I can't believe you just said that."

"I can't believe you can't believe it." Emma folded her arms under her breasts and scowled. "What's the matter, Max, never been turned down before?"

"Why are you being such a pain in the ass?" Max turned to her, frustration written all over his face. "I offer to help you, buy you dinner, kiss you senseless and bring you to orgasm, oh, no, don't bother lying about that either," he yelled as she opened her mouth, "and all you do is give me grief!"

"You felt me up without permission, kidnapped me, practically attacked me on the street, *bit me*, then act like a crazy man, drive like a bat out of hell out of town, and you want to know why I'm giving you grief? You're lucky I haven't broken out the mace, pal!"

"All I want to know is who hurt you!" he yelled at the top of his lungs.

"It happened two years ago, Max! What are you gonna do, hunt the guy down in jail and beat him up?"

"Ah-hah!" Max's finger waved in her face. "Someone *did* hurt you!"

"Argh!" Emma's hands flew into the air in frustration. "All right! I was mugged, okay? It was a college student, he's in jail, I had a broken wrist but he got a broken nose, end of story!"

Emma glared at him, her arms crossed over her chest. If he made one wrong move, hell, one wrong *sound*, she *would* mace him!

He grinned as the temper visibly drained out of him. "Did you give him as much grief as you've given me?"

"*More.*"

"God, you are so beautiful when you're pissed." He grabbed the back of her head and gave her a quick, hard kiss. "Okay, warrior princess, now that you've told me what I wanted to know I'll tell you what you want to know. Okay?"

Emma took a deep breath and debated whether or not to kiss him back or clobber him. "It better be good."

Max leaned in until her lips were once more beneath his. "And then I'm going to take you home and fuck you raw." As her eyes widened, he added, "And, baby, that will be better than good."

She was completely speechless as he got out of the SUV in a slow glide that had her thinking of silk sheets and heated skin. She gulped as he prowled around the hood of the Durango, moving like sex in jeans. His heated gaze never left her face.

"Oh, boy," she whispered as he opened her car door. He smiled when he saw her seat belt was still on.

He reached in slowly to unhook her seat belt, brushing his arm deliberately against her breasts. Her nipples hardened, rasping against his sleeve as he removed his arm just as slowly. His smile, sexy and satisfied, showed he'd felt it.

Suddenly, she had to know. "Max?"

"Hmm?"

She ignored the hand he held out to help her down. "Why me?" He looked confused. "I mean, you just came home three months ago and can still have any woman in Halle. Why are you trying to seduce *me*?"

"The real question in my mind is why I didn't try it sooner."

Emma stared into his eyes, reading regrets past and a determination that almost alarmed her. When he cocked his brow questioningly, she took his hand and let him help her out of the Durango. She took a deep breath to steady herself. "Okay, what's the big deal?"

Max's lips twitched.

Emma crossed her arms and tapped her foot. Her chin lifted as she waited for an answer.

Max reached out and gently stroked the bite mark on her neck. "Do you remember how you felt when I bit you there?"

Remember? My legs still feel like rubber. She nodded, doing her best not to let any of that show in her face while secretly locking her knees. She must not have succeeded because Max's smile heated. "That was me marking you as mine."

Emma rolled her eyes. "Didn't we have this discussion, Captain Caveman? A hickey does not make me yours."

"But in this case, it does." When Emma shook her head, he

nodded. "There's a special enzyme that's only released when I bite someone. I released it into you, Emma. You're my mate."

"Doesn't it take three bites to turn me, Dracula?" She didn't even bother trying to keep the disbelief out of either her face or her voice.

"If I was a vampire, yes, it would." Max grinned, his eyes glinting oddly in the moonlight.

"Oh. So I'm going to start baying at the moon, then." She nodded sagely.

"No, baby, you're going to purr," he purred, licking his mark with a rough, raspy tongue.

Emma shivered. "You know, this has to be the oddest way a man's tried to get in my pants in ages."

He snarled warningly, the sound oddly cat-like and strangely familiar. "Didn't we say we wouldn't discuss you and other men?"

"Max, you're not making any sense. Now, let me call Simon and we can discuss getting your Thorazine prescription renewed..."

Max strangled a laugh, lifting his head from her neck. "Look at my eyes, Emma."

She looked. Then she blinked. She opened her mouth to say something, *anything,* but nothing came out. His eyes had turned to pure molten gold, shining in the moonlight with an eerie luminescence that one only saw in the eyes of...cats.

"Contact lenses?" she asked weakly.

He shook his head and blinked, his eyes that quickly turning back to sunshine blue.

"You're a, what? Werecat?"

"Puma, actually."

"Puma," she repeated weakly, dropping back to lean

against the Durango's door. "And you bit me, so now I'm going to roar at the full moon?"

He sighed. "Actually, Pumas can't roar, we're missing the necessary parts. Specialized larynx and hyoid apparatus, to be precise. And we can change at will, we aren't ruled by the moon."

"Oh." Emma's head was reeling. "Can you show me?"

Max frowned. "Show you?"

"Yeah." Emma straightened up, half terrified and half excited at the prospect of seeing him change. She waved her hand at him commandingly. "Change. Become a cat."

"Now?"

"Yeah, now! What, you need to wait for the full moon? I thought you said you could change at will?"

"Emma—"

"I mean, why tell me this at all if you weren't willing to, I dunno, *prove* it or something?"

"Emma—"

He was starting to sound all snarly again. "So c'mon, Lion-O, hop to it." She clapped, loud and sharp. "Chop-chop!"

"Emma!"

"What?"

"Have you ever seen a cougar in Levi's?"

"No."

"Neither have I." He looked like he couldn't decide if he wanted to laugh or yowl.

"You mean you'd have to..." Emma eyed his jeans speculatively.

"*Yes.*"

"Oh."

"And if my ass is naked, baby, you'd better believe yours will be too."

Emma put her hands on her hips and glared at him. "Isn't this why you brought me all the way out here, to show me your Incredible Cougar Act?"

"Puma."

"Whatever."

"No."

"Then why?"

"I figured if you screamed no one would hear you."

Emma blinked. "Gee, Max, you're all heart." He had the grace to blush. "So, because you bit me, and released your enzyme thingy in me, I'm going to change into a puma?"

Max nodded.

"Does it hurt?"

Max shook his head. His eyes had glued themselves to her neck, the hunger in them getting stronger by the second.

"When?"

"When what?" he asked absently, his hand drifting down to her arm before moving to stroke the bite mark.

"When will I change, Max?"

"I changed within the first forty-eight hours after I got bit."

Emma gasped in sympathetic horror. "Is that why you left and never came back, Max? Because you got bit?"

"No, I was bit because I was next in line to be Alpha."

Emma shook her head. "Okay, now I'm *totally* confused. Maybe I've got food poisoning from my seafood alfredo and I'm actually in the hospital having hallucinations and heaving into a bucket," she muttered.

Max laughed as he focused once again on her face. "Want

me to prove you're wide awake?" One hand snaked out, gently cupping her breast. His thumb raked across her nipple, shooting sparks straight down to her clit.

"Oh boy," Emma whispered. "Okay, I'm awake." She pulled reluctantly away from his caressing hand, determined to focus on the whole Emma-as-a-cat thing. With growing confusion, she rubbed at her forehead. "Can you please explain before my brain explodes?"

"Jonathon Friedelinde was Alpha before me. His daughter didn't show Alpha tendencies, so a competition was held to determine who was strong enough to be the next Alpha. Simon and I overheard Marie and some of her friends whispering about the competition and we both entered, not knowing what the hell we were getting into, or what the prize was. Jonathon forgot to make the contest Puma only, which I pointed out to him with great, annoying frequency until he relented and let us in." Max shrugged. "I came in first, Simon came in second. What really bothered some people was the fact that Simon and I were both still human when we won, against some who'd been Pumas since childhood."

"So you knew about the Pumas even before you entered the contest?"

"I was friends with Marie for years, saw her change once."

Emma stared at him in growing horror, thinking of all the ways a Puma could rip into a man. "You could have been killed!"

Max seemed completely unconcerned. "If it had been a duel to the death, yeah, we both would have died. Instead it was a test of endurance, intelligence and cunning, and probably the most fun either of us has ever had. And sometimes I think the only reason we won was because no one was allowed to shift."

"What was the test, paintball? Capture the flag?"

Max grinned. “Something like that, but a lot more complicated.” Max reached out and wrapped his hand around the nape of her neck, seemingly unable to go for any length of time without touching her somehow. The gesture was surprisingly comforting. “Jonathon bit us both that night, to our surprise. I was twenty, Simon nineteen.”

She reached up and gently stroked his cheek. “And confused as all hell, I’ll bet.”

He leaned into her caress, his eyes closing in pleasure. “We got used to it, and as soon as Jonathon stepped down I came home and named Simon my Beta.”

“Beta?”

“Mm-hmm, my second-in-command.”

“You said I’m your mate,” Emma whispered as Max pulled her into his arms.

“My Curana.”

“Your who-wadda?”

She could feel Max’s laughter rumbling through his chest. “My Curana. Mate to the Alpha. It’s supposedly a name derived from the Portuguese word for cougar.”

“Oh.”

Emma allowed Max to pull her head gently to his chest. She snuggled into his warmth, inhaling his unique scent, oddly comforted by his presence. “So,” he rumbled, “we’ve done the dinner and fight.” He leaned down and kissed the top of her head. “Come home with me, little Curana. I want to make love to you. I want to be inside you the next time you come.”

Emma shivered as she heard the low, rumbling purr emanating from him. “Max?”

“Hmm?” His hand started to stroke up and down her back, gently nudging her towards the SUV.

"Will I have to use a litter box?"

"Emma!"

Chapter Four

Max took his time driving her home. He wanted to savor having her next to him for as long as possible. "Do you open tomorrow, or does Becky?"

Emma turned towards him. She'd been far away, and he'd left her to her thoughts. After all, he'd dumped a remarkable amount of information on her in a short amount of time, and she'd handled it remarkably well. He was so proud of her he was ready to burst with it.

"Actually, I close tomorrow and Becky opens. Becks closes Saturday."

Max smiled in pure anticipation. "Good. We can take our time tonight. Adrian's got the early morning, I have late shift."

Her shiver of response was enough to send heat flooding his system.

"Emma?"

"Hmm?"

He was truly curious about the calm way she'd responded to everything he'd thrown at her so far., "You took everything I told you really well."

"I've never understood the woe-is-me thing. I mean, the hottest guy in town just told me he wants me badly enough to bite me and make me like him, and now he wants to drag me home and ravish me. I'm going to, what, run screaming into the night? Oh, no! I'm a Puma now! My life is over! Sob!" Emma rolled her eyes. "I mean, don't get me wrong, it's still freaking me out a bit, and it's probably going to cost me a fortune in bikini waxing, but it's not the end of my world."

Max nearly ran off the road. "You get a bikini wax?"

"Wouldn't you like to know?"

"Hell yes."

Her laughter filled up all the empty places inside him he hadn't even known were there.

"If Simon and Becky get together, does that mean he'll bite her?"

Max nodded. "If he wants to mate her, he'll have to bite her. And from what he told me, he wants to mate her."

Emma gave him a speculative look out of the corner of her eye. "How many women have you bitten?"

"As a mate, or to turn?"

Emma growled, startled at how possessive she felt. "How many mates do you have?"

"Only one, Curana." He took his hand off the steering wheel to stroke the back of her neck soothingly.

Emma still glared at him. "And how many women have you turned?"

"Two, not counting you."

"Oh?"

Max grinned at her possessive tone. "One as a favor to Jonathon, one because it was the only way I could think of to fix a problem she had. And, no, I can't explain it further than that; it's not my secret to tell."

"Did you have sex with the women you turned?" His slight

wince was all the answer she needed. "Who?"

"Emma..."

"*Who?* Livia."

Max sighed. "Livia."

Emma groaned. "How did I know you were going to say that?"

"What can I say? I was young and stupid."

"Was she the favor or the problem?"

"Jonathon asked me to turn her. Maybe he thought, since Marie and I didn't hit it off, that Livia would turn out to be my mate."

"Especially since the two of you were already doing the mattress mambo?"

Max flushed. "We broke up soon after that."

Emma remembered the circumstances of the break up, and winced. "So it had nothing to do with how she insulted me," she muttered, not thinking about how that would sound.

"It had everything to do with how she insulted you." When she looked at him, confused, he smiled. It wasn't pleasant. "She was very good at hiding how much of a bitch she really is. I broke up with her that night over what she said about you, and what she wanted to do about Becky's punch stunt." He shuddered. "She's been on my tail since I got back into town. So far nothing I've done has gotten her to leave me alone." Max's smile was cheerful. "But I have the feeling you won't have that problem."

Max turned into his driveway and pressed the button to open the garage door. He lived in a lovely historic house his parents had left to him when they retired to Florida. The home was craftsman in style, built early in the twentieth century, and had been lovingly restored by the entire Cannon family. The dark gray gable roof was set off by rich mahogany brown shingles and bright white trim work, with rich red fieldstone set around the base of the house. The front had that beautiful pillar and post design, with a covered porch that wrapped around to the left side of the house. The elder Cannons had added on a two-car garage and utility room to the right side of the house. They'd made the extension look like just another part of the house by having the garage entrance on the side rather than the front. The windows along the front matched the rest of the house. Emma had never been inside, but she'd always admired it from afar.

Max pulled into the garage and turned off the Durango. He reached up and pressed a button, closing the garage door behind them. He turned to her with a solemn joy that startled her.

"Welcome home, Curana."

Emma opened her mouth to reply, but he was already getting out of the SUV. She hopped out on her own, ignoring the amused shake of his head. He waited for her to round the hood of the car before opening the door into the utility room.

She started to step through the door but he startled her. With a swift move he picked her up, ignoring her gasp of surprise. He carried her into the utility room. "Get the door, will you?"

She reached out with a foot and kicked the door shut.

He laughed. "The other one."

She leaned down and opened the door into the rest of the house.

He carried her into a kitchen straight out of her fantasies. It was laid out in a u-shape with simple arts and crafts style cherry cabinets with silver handles. Stainless steel appliances gleamed in the gentle light Max had left on, their lines set off by the beautiful black granite countertops. Cherry hardwood covered the floors from the kitchen into the breakfast area off on the right where a round table and four Shaker-style chairs sat. The windows in the breakfast nook ran nearly floor to ceiling, with a simple geometric design set into the top panel. He'd painted the walls a rich sage green and the traditional trim around the windows a bright white.

Without pausing, Max carried her through the kitchen, past the breakfast nook and into the great room. The sage green walls, cherry floors and white trim carried through into this room. A vaulted ceiling with skylights gave the room the feeling of being huge. A large reddish brown leather sofa dominated the great room. It rested on a bold area rug done in a geometric pattern of reds, blacks and greens. It faced a set of built-in cherry cabinets along one wall that doubled as the entertainment center with bookshelves on either side. The fireplace, on the opposite wall, was decorated with the same fieldstone that was outside the house. She caught a glimpse of the huge double doors at the front of the house before Max carried her past the fireplace down a short corridor and through another door.

A king size cherry wood sleigh bed dominated the room. It was covered in a crazy quilt of geometric designs in bold blues, reds and blacks. He'd painted the walls a warm terra cotta, with framed black and white prints by Escher, whimsical brain twisters that would normally capture her attention but, now, barely registered.

She could make out the master bathroom through the open doorway, barely. The cabinets in there appeared to match the ones in the kitchen, but the room was dominated by the massive oval tub, surrounded by rich, highly polished tumbled stones inset with black ceramic diamonds. The same tumbled stone was on the floor. The room had been painted a dark red wine color.

Emma realized Max had stopped moving. Looking up at him, she found him staring down at her with a quizzical look. "Well?"

Emma blushed. She'd been rubbernecking in Max's house, trying to take in everything at once. "It's incredible."

He smiled with satisfaction. "If there's anything you want to change, you'll have to let me know." Gently he placed her on the quilt. "This is now as much your house as mine."

Emma's mouth fell open as he toed off his shoes and socks. "You're kidding me, right?"

Max began unbuttoning his shirt, diverting her attention from his whole "*Mi casa es su casa*" attitude. "I was in Simon's shop when you called about the Madonna, you know."

"Oh. Really?" she replied absently. She could barely speak as Max unveiled the finest chest it had ever been her privilege to see. It was lightly sprinkled with light brown hairs, trailing down his stomach to point directly into his pants. Dark brown nipples peeped out from the hair, tempting her into some very sinful thoughts.

"Yes, I was. And you know what?"

Emma didn't know her own name; Max was unbuttoning his jeans. "Um, nope."

"You live up to your voice," Max purred as he slipped his jeans down his legs.

"Urgh," Emma choked, "naked." She could feel her eyes bugging out of her head. Max went commando. A sinful buffet of man-flesh was laid out before her in one single sweep of his hands. She didn't know whether to sigh or to sob.

"Yes, I am." Max laughed huskily. "Now it's your turn."

Emma bit her lip, a sudden attack of shyness nearly

paralyzing her. Max didn't know it yet, but he'd be her first, and from the look on his face she'd better tell him soon.

"Max?" Emma sat there, her hands clenched in her lap, her gaze riveted to his cock. The thing looked huge, all veined and red, and pointed straight at her. A small drop of liquid seeped from the slit. It twitched a salute to her rapt attention.

"Yes, Emma?"

Her gaze lifted to his; unknown to her, they'd turned pure, molten gold. "You remember the talk of other men?"

He growled low in his throat and crawled onto the bed.

"Eep," she whispered, lying down as he prowled up her body.

"You were saying?" he whispered huskily as he settled his naked body between her thighs. He brushed against her cheek with his lips, a caress so soft she barely felt it. It sent a shiver down her spine. Those same lips continued their incredible journey, trailing down the side of her neck to settle on the bite he'd given her outside the restaurant. Goose bumps raced up and down her arms as he moved his hips in a sinuous motion, brushing his naked cock against her mound.

"Um, there weren't," she squeaked, unconsciously arching up into his body as he scrapped his teeth along his mark.

"Weren't what?" he muttered, one hand moving up to start sliding her camisole up her stomach. He paused long enough to caress her there, trailing fire in his wake.

"Any other men."

His hand stopped.

His mouth stopped.

His hips stopped. She was really sad when his hips stopped.

"You're a virgin?" His voice sounded oddly strangled.

"It's not a crime to be one, you know. I'm not the Oldest Living Virgin, or anything. It's not like I'm in the Guinness Book of World Records," she babbled. "Besides, I've done other things…oh!" His hands had started moving again, with a swiftness that startled her. Her camisole was toast as he ripped it literally from her body, his claws barely scraping her skin, sending shivers of need once again down her spine.

Claws?

Emma had barely registered the fact that Max had used his *claws* to ruin her favorite shirt when he started working on her jeans. "No! Bad kitty!" She slapped him on the top of his head, determined to save at least some of her wardrobe.

He lifted his head, his eyes golden and burning, a rumbling sound emanating from his throat as he pinned her hands above her head. Emma thought about struggling, but something about the way he looked had her lying passively. "You're a virgin."

Emma blinked, unsure how to respond. "Duh."

Max stared down at her, his eyes narrowing as he studied her features as if seeing her for the very first time. "No man has ever touched you."

She thought about telling him about the make-out sessions her one and only boyfriend had talked her into, the oral sex they'd indulged in a few times, but decided that discretion was the better part of valor. Jimmy was a nice guy, and deserved to live. "Again. Duh."

"No man will ever touch you again."

Emma studied granite-like features above her. "Even you?" The growl deepened. She sighed, inexplicably happy to hear that sound. "Okay." She rolled her eyes. "Duh." She grinned. "By the way, Lion-O, that was my favorite shirt."

He looked down. "Damn, Emma."

"What?" She looked down, expecting to see something odd, like dried alfredo sauce decorating one boob or something. Instead she saw the pale pink lace bra she'd put on that morning, the one that was completely see-through. It helped give her confidence to feel the sexy lingerie against her skin, so much so she'd replaced all of her old undies with the lacy stuff.

From the look, and feel, of things, Max definitely approved.

Max switched her wrists into one hand. The other trailed down her body to her jeans, undoing the snap and zipper with ease. "Lift your ass, Emma," he commanded. She obeyed without thinking, shifting so he could ease her jeans down her legs.

He hissed out a breath at the sight of the pale pink lace panties that matched the bra. Underneath, she was hairless. "A full Brazilian," he sighed.

"Uh-huh."

He moved his hand and began petting her over her panties, cupping her intimately. "Mine," he sighed. His golden eyes bored into hers, a silent command in them. "Keep your hands where they are."

"Why?" Emma complied as Max moved his hand slowly from her wrists, trailing down her arm to the side of her breast.

"Because I'm not ready for you to touch me yet. I want this first time to be yours."

"I'd rather it was ours." She gasped as his hand gently embraced her breast. His thumb strummed gently over her nipple, causing it to peak under the pink bra.

"Trust me, Curana. The pleasure will be ours." Slowly, oh so slowly, Max lowered his head. His tongue snaked out and licked over her nipple through the lace, watching her reactions as she gasped softly. "I'm going to get you naked now, Emma." He lifted his head from her breast. "Leave your hands where they are. Remember, Emma."

Max gently pulled the cups of her bra down, resting her breasts on the lowered cups until they looked like an offering laid out on pink lace. He bent and suckled one nipple into his mouth, stroking it with his tongue until she writhed against him, panting and moaning in need. He switched to the other nipple, suckling and nipping with such force it was nearly painful. Emma panted, damn near coming from the sensation.

He pulled away from her. "Uh-uh, little Emma," he purred. "No coming unless I'm in you, remember?"

She groaned as he moved down her body. His hands went to her lacy panties, thumbs hooking under the band. With slow deliberation he pulled them from her body, slowly exposing her to his hot gaze. "You were right, Emma, to stop me before." He looked up with a grin that made her moan. "I'd forgotten how much fun it is to play with my food."

And with that, Max began a sensuous torture that had her writhing with need.

He began by slowly nibbling his way up her left leg, starting at her ankle and ending at her inner thigh, right next to her pussy lips. He then switched sides, once again kissing and nibbling his way up her leg until she was practically begging him to eat her.

When she felt the first hot swipe of his tongue on her pussy she came, screaming his name. With a purring rumble, he continued to lap at her until her orgasm subsided, the vibrations making the orgasm that much more intense. "Naughty, Emma. I wasn't inside you."

"Whoops." Emma looked down at him with a lopsided grin.

"I'm pleased you've left your hands in place, though. So maybe, this time, I'll forgo punishing you."

Emma blinked. "And once again, Captain Caveman rears

his ugly head," she gasped. Max had started rubbing her clit in oh-so-gentle circles, bringing her arousal back to near peak. "Max," she sighed, her hips moving in time to his hand.

"Do you want to come, Emma?" Max asked, the heat in his gaze damn near burning her.

"Yes," she sighed again, licking her lips as she stared down at him. "Please, Max."

He shivered slightly. Then his rough tongue was once again on her clit, licking and nibbling as she gasped and moaned beneath his mouth. His finger had moved to her opening, circling slowly until finally settling inside her. He stroked her gently, matching his rhythm there to the movements of her body. His finger curved slightly, and Emma saw stars.

"Come, Emma," he whispered, using his thumb to stroke her clit as his finger picked up speed. She didn't even mind when he inserted a second finger; she was too busy seeing stars as her climax hit her with the force of a freight train.

When she came down from it, Max was gently stroking her soaking wet pussy. She opened her eyes to find he'd moved so that he lay next to her. With a satisfied smile, she pulled him down, kissing him lovingly. She could taste herself on his lips, and it added an element of eroticism she'd never felt before.

"I'm going to take you now, Emma."

Emma shivered. She licked her lips, her body tensing slightly with nerves. "Okay."

"Shhh." He kissed her again, gentle and loving as he moved his body between her thighs. "I will never willingly hurt you, Emma."

"I know," she whispered, awed. This was Max, the only man who'd ever held her heart, and he was claiming her for his own. She gently clasped his shoulders as he began to slowly invade her body, his cock stretching her open. The slight burning pain caused her to dig her nails in. She bit her lip and forced herself to relax as much as humanly possible while slowly being invaded by a red-hot iron bar.

"So tight," he gasped as he finally seated himself all the way inside her.

"Were your parents psychic?" Emma asked, gulping a little at the sting of his invasion.

Max frowned down at her, confused. "No, why?"

"Are you sure? I mean, with a name like Max Cannon—"

"*Emma!*"

"Sorry, but from the feel of things that can't be a small caliber you've got shoved up there, boyo."

Max leaned down, resting his forehead against hers as he started to laugh shakily. "I love you, Emma."

"Oh boy," she breathed as he slowly began to move.

"Is that all you can say?" He was grinning down at her knowingly, as if he had no doubts as to what her answer would be.

Emma felt all her old insecurities come to the fore, even as his cock had her gasping in pleasure. "Are you sure?"

He stopped, leaning down to kiss her thoroughly. "I'm sure."

She stared into his face, reading the love there, the heat, the need. With deliberate slowness she raised her arms above her head and grasped the headboard. She lifted her head out and to the side in an instinctive show of submission, giving him her throat, accepting him fully. "Fuck me, Max."

Max lost control for the first time in his adult life. His teeth bit into his mark as he began pounding into her body with little finesse. He fucked her into the mattress, and she loved every minute of it. She wrapped her legs around his waist and held on for dear life as he once again sent her over the edge, her climax so strong she nearly passed out. The clenching of her body was enough to bring him off, his semen pouring into her in a tidal wave of wet heat. With a gasp that was almost a sob he collapsed on top of her, his breathing harsh and uneven, his heart pounding.

"I love you too," she whispered, cuddling him close as he began to purr.

Chapter Five

Max woke with the most incredible feeling of well being he'd ever experienced in his life. Emma was curled up against him, his arms around her protectively as she slept. Her luscious backside was nestled firmly against his morning erection, a situation Max totally approved of. Her scent was all over him, as his was all over her. His hips bucked forward involuntarily and he moaned as her hot, slick flesh stroked the head of his penis. God, he hoped she liked morning sex. And afternoon sex. And evening sex...

"Morning, Max." Her voice was amused, rough from sleep and sexy as hell.

"For the love of God, please tell me you aren't sore," he whispered, practically begging.

Emma leaned up on one elbow, twisting around to stare at him. She wound up partially on her stomach, and Max's eyes immediately zeroed in on that incredible ass of hers. "Not much, but honestly, other...issues...need to be taken care of first." She blushed slightly.

Max looked at her uncomfortable face and grinned. "Bathroom's that way."

She was up and out of the bed before he'd finished pointing, sprinting naked across the room. Max leaned back and enjoyed the brief view he was given before the bathroom door shut behind her. He snickered when he heard her sigh of relief. He was grinning as he climbed out of bed and snagged his jeans.

"You want coffee?" he yelled through the bathroom door just as she flushed.

She opened the door, peeking around the edge. "You have tea?"

He thought for a moment, frowning, running a mental inventory of what his mother may have left behind on her last visit. "I have Darjeeling, Earl Grey and Spiced Chai."

"Spiced Chai, sweet, with cream?"

"Coming right up. Borrow my toothbrush; we'll pick up your stuff from your apartment later today." He ignored her sudden frown and walked out of the room. He slipped his jeans on once he was in the hall and made his way to the kitchen. He whistled cheerfully as he began making her tea and his coffee, setting both machines to working as he contemplated what to make his prickly little mate for breakfast. He pulled out the eggs, knowing he could at least make scrambled eggs and toast without looking like a total idiot in the kitchen.

"You owe me a shirt, Lion-O."

He turned, his cock hardening as he saw his shirt on her. It practically swallowed her whole, and she looked damn fine in it. It didn't hurt that she wasn't wearing anything beneath it. Her tousled hair and kiss-swollen lips completed the just-fucked look.

Then he looked into her eyes and nearly dropped the eggs.

Her eyes gleamed gold, full of heat and passion. He felt his own flare in response, his gaze raking her from head to toe as he prowled towards her, the eggs left behind on the counter. "Emma," he purred, wrapping his hands around her waist.

"Hmm?" She stroked his chest with her small hands, fingers tangling in the hairs on his chest.

He leaned down and lapped at his mark, groaning when she bared her throat. "You're changing."

"What?" she asked absently, her hands moving towards the snap of his jeans. "You taste so good," she whispered, licking his neck with a tongue turned raspy.

Max shivered. "Emma," he groaned as her teeth nipped at his neck. Her canines had grown in. "You're changing, sweetheart."

"Thought you said I had two days," she muttered as her hand worked its way inside his pants. With a happy sigh she stroked his shaft, pulling it out of his jeans to run her thumb over the head.

Max moaned, ready to push her down on the table and take her swift and hard. That could be a problem if she shifted before they were done. "Emma, you have to stop."

"Who says?" She knelt in front of him and took his cock in her mouth, sucking lightly on the head, her tongue rasping along the slit. "Mmm, you do taste good." She licked her lips, teasing and seductive.

Max stared down at her, fighting his own instincts. He wanted to thrust between her lips, hold her head in place while he fucked her there, make sure she swallowed every last bit of him.

But she was changing. It was up to him to act responsibly. He was Alpha, it was his job to protect her, and...

She'd wrapped her lips around his cock again, licking up and down the shaft, her head bobbing in a steady rhythm that would soon have him coming down her throat. With a snarl, the Puma took over as he grabbed the sides of her head and held her in place for his pleasure.

"That's it, baby, use your tongue," he growled, watching her pleasure him as his hips moved slowly, sliding his shaft between her lips. She curled that wicked tongue slightly, rasping it against the throbbing vein, catching the flared edge.

One of his hands moved to the back of her head, gently bunching her hair in his fist in a show of dominance as the Alpha in him took over. He could feel chills run up and down his spine as his climax neared, but he kept his rhythm steady, trying not to choke her while forcing her to take everything she could. He crooned to her, telling her how wonderful her hot mouth felt against him, how beautiful she was to him.

He moved the hand not holding her hair to just under her chin as he felt her incisors turn sharp. "Suck, Emma," he commanded, his power flowing free as he lost control, his climax almost on him.

She gave him a teasing flick of her tongue before she obeyed, her cheeks hollowing out as she sucked on the head of his cock, pulling the orgasm out of him as she increased her purr at the same time. He erupted into her mouth, back arched, head thrown back as his cry of completion came out more like the primal snarl of his Puma. His mate took everything he gave her, swallowing him down as he held her head in place.

With a final, rumbling purr, she licked him clean then stood. She gently tucked his softening cock back into his jeans, zipping and snapping them shut before she gently patted his chest.

"You still owe me a shirt, Lion-O." With a wicked grin, she sauntered off to the bedroom, her ass swaying beneath his shirt. Max grinned, eggs forgotten, and followed her into the bedroom.

Emma felt edgy all day. She'd had yet another fight with

Max, insisting on going to work that afternoon and giving Becky her allotted evening off. She could feel the Puma crawling under her skin, trying to break free; Max had warned her what could happen if she allowed the change to occur without him present. Like she wanted to change into a mountain lion in the middle of her store! He'd grumbled all the way to her apartment, the entire time she changed clothes, and all the way to Wallflowers. By the time he dropped her off, she was ready to bite him, and not in a good way. She felt caged, pacing the storeroom when she wasn't waiting on customers. She'd managed to keep her eyes from changing, a trick Max had taught her quickly when he realized she wouldn't give in. He'd also told her he would be picking her up after work. She agreed with him that she was in no condition to drive.

She barely made it through the day, closing an hour early and leaving the receipts for Becky. She needed more room to pace, more room to...run.

Emma walked the six blocks to Max's office. Both Adrian and Max were there, as was the receptionist, Lisa Pryce. Emma waved hello to a puzzled Lisa before sitting in the waiting area, tapping her foot impatiently.

Adrian Giordano walked out of one of the examination rooms, talking quietly to Livia Patterson. She looked thoroughly disgusted, completely ignoring the hunky doctor as he tried his best to get her to pay attention. Adrian spoke to the receptionist as Livia, without even a glance at Emma, flounced out of the office.

"Emma?"

"Hi, Adrian." Emma smiled tightly. "Was Livia upset she got you instead of Max?"

Adrian grinned. "So Max told you about her attempts to get to him?"

Emma had a hard time not baring her teeth. She wanted to rip Livia's heart out. It took all of the self-control she had to keep her eyes brown instead of gold. "Yup."

Adrian coughed, turning away abruptly. "Max? Emma's here."

"Emma?" She could hear his muffled voice from behind one of the examination room doors. It opened abruptly and a frowning Max stepped out, followed by the elderly Mrs. Roman. "Why didn't you wait at your shop for me?"

Emma grinned at him, her expression tight, her body strung out. Her foot jiggled impatiently. It felt like the worst caffeine high she'd ever been on. Her skin itched and crawled, her gums ached, and her eyes hurt with the effort to keep them brown.

"Oh." Max sighed and turned to Mrs. Roman. "Here's your prescription, and a copy for your records, Lena. Why don't you have Lisa help you pick out a pair of frames? We can see to it that they're sent off to the lab first thing in the morning."

Mrs. Roman grinned wickedly. "Hot date, Max?" She waggled her eyebrows at him when he merely smiled smugly. "Taking Emma out, eh?"

"Yes, ma'am." Max smiled and winked at Emma, who had to bite her lip to keep from snarling.

"Well, you take good care of her, you hear? From what Jimmy said, she's a keeper." Max's grin froze on his face. "You mark my words, if you haven't snapped her up by the time he gets back this way, he'll steal her back out from under you."

"Who's Jimmy?" Max asked. His tone was pleasant, his expression wasn't.

"Jimmy was Emma's boyfriend until about four months ago when he had to leave town to deal with some family issues. Rumor has it he's headed back this way any day now. Who knows? He might give you some competition!"

Emma groaned and put her head in her hands as Max's attention swung back towards her. "We broke up two months before he left town, Mrs. Roman."

"Not to hear Jimmy tell it, you didn't," Mrs. Roman replied with a laugh.

"I'll just have to make sure Jimmy knows Emma's taken." Max's hands went to his hips as he took in Emma's red cheeks and guilty eyes.

Mrs. Roman cackled with glee; she was the biggest gossip in town, and Max had just handed her a prime piece to chew on.

"Can you do me a favor, Mrs. Roman? Can you wait to tell anyone that Emma and I are together until the masquerade party on Saturday? We want to surprise a few people." Max smiled down at the elderly woman, using all of his not inconsiderable charm.

"Those few people being Olivia Patterson and Belinda Campbell?" When Max merely shrugged, Mrs. Roman grinned. "Max, anything that will make Livia and Belinda squirm is okay by me. But..." she wagged her finger under his nose, ignoring his little boy grin, "...you have only until Saturday!"

She was so happy she forgot to wait around and pick out the frames for her new glasses, heading straight out the door with an absent wave good-bye. Emma knew the story of Max's declaration would be all over town by mid-afternoon Saturday. She stared right at a smug Max, torn between laughing and screaming. "Happy, Captain Caveman?"

Adrian's choked laugh and Lisa's snort of amusement broke the tie. Emma laughed up at Max, who was still grinning like a schoolboy.

"You okay to close up, Adrian?"

"Can you give me just five minutes before you head out? I have a question about Mr. Davis."

Max looked over at Emma, who was practically dancing in her seat, and back at Adrian. He nodded, clearly torn. "Hey, Emma? Can you wait in here for me? I'll just be a few minutes, okay?"

Emma huffed and followed him into an examination room. He kissed her quickly and closed the door behind him. The room was typical of eye exam rooms everywhere, with a black examination chair and all of the equipment surrounding it. A desk sat in one corner of the room off to the side of the chair. A mirror on one wall showed the letter "E" when she turned the lights off.

Emma paced, her skin twitching. She rubbed her arms briskly, trying not to scratch. She felt like she could peel her own skin off. Sure enough, when she looked down at her hands she saw claws where her nails should be.

"Ah, hell." She ran to the mirror and looked in it. Gold eyes stared back at her. She licked her lips, feeling the edges of fangs as her tongue went back in her mouth. Scenes from *Teen Wolf* were going through her mind as she desperately tried to stay human.

She gave up when the fur started sprouting.

Max entered the examination room, not terribly surprised to see the Puma in his examination chair. The cat was sitting in a pair of blue jeans and a red lightweight sweater, the same clothes Emma had been wearing when she entered the office. It looked adorably pissed.

Max leaned against the doorjamb and sighed, desperately trying not to laugh. "I told you not to go into work today."

She snarled at him. She kept snarling at him as he

untangled her from her clothes. She quietly snarled at him as he led her to his SUV, which he pulled in behind the office so he could sneak her into it. She snarled the whole way out of town.

She was still snarling at him when he led her into the woods. She stopped snarling when he got naked. When he changed, she began purring.

With a playful flick of her tail she invited him to chase her.

She purred loudest of all when he caught her.

Chapter Six

"You expect me to wear that?" Emma looked at the picture on the bag of the most incredibly X-rated (okay, maybe high-R) pirate outfit she'd ever seen. All the model needed was a half-naked pirate next to her to make the picture complete. The frilly, lacy cream skirt hit the girl just before full exposure; God forbid if the poor thing tried to sit, she'd be showing her assets to everyone in the room! The girl's breasts spilled out of the matching top, helped along by a burgundy waist cinch with an attached overskirt. The cinch and skirt combo was embroidered in an elaborate design done in gold. Lace bell sleeves allowed her hands freedom while promising to drip into everything. The feathered hat matched the cinch, with the edges decorated in creamy lace. No less than four feathers peeked around the rim of the hat. Tall black boots with three-inch heels and a remarkably lifelike saber completed the outfit. If Max thought she'd wear the lacy thigh-high stockings he'd bought, he was in for a rude awakening. The stockings definitely took the outfit into X-land.

Max's innocent expression didn't fool her for a moment. There was simply no way he could hide the heat in his eyes. "It matches my costume. Besides, the model in that thing has to be taller than you. The skirt should hit you mid-thigh."

"Oh, yes, that makes it *so* much better."

They were sitting in Max's breakfast nook, finishing the last of their coffee. Emma needed to open the store that day; Becky would close at five. Emma planned on handing Becky her costume just before she left for the day, leaving Becky no option but to wear what Max had provided since the masquerade was that night. Although, looking at the costume he'd chosen for her, she was a little leery about the costume he'd gotten for her friend. "Who picked out Becky's costume?"

"Simon."

"Oh boy. Can I see the costume she's probably going to throw at my head?"

Max grinned and reached into the bag he'd brought to the table that morning. He pulled out an off-the-shoulder black lacy top with long sleeves that were tight at the arms and flared out at the wrists. Next he pulled out a black skirt. It was short and flaring, the kind that would fly up if you spun in place. On top of the skirt he laid out a leather belt with a silver belt buckle, a swordsman's belt meant for a real rapier. Tall black boots almost identical to Emma's, a black bandito hat, black cape and black mask completed the outfit. Where Emma's outfit was blatantly sexy, Becky's was sexy in an understated way. Her skirt would probably hit her mid-thigh as well, but in all other respects she was almost modestly covered, especially since it was obvious the cape would hit her at her knees, thus covering her dignity in back. Unlike Emma's outfit, which took dignity and kicked its ass to the curb with a cheery wave and a fond farewell.

"Wow. I'm impressed. I should have let Simon pick my outfit, too."

Emma grinned at the sound of Max's low-pitched, possessive growl.

"Okay, so..." Emma folded her hands on top of Becky's

costume, "...where's my outfit for the party? I mean, I have to assume this outfit is for, like, role-playing at home or something."

"I am going to show the entire world exactly how sexy I find you." His hands covered hers, both soothing her and locking her into place. Gold flecks danced in the blue of his eyes and Emma shivered. "No one will doubt how much I want you. I plan on having every single male there drooling with envy that I'm the one who has you. I want every female there to hate you on sight."

"Just being with you will do that," Emma muttered.

Max grinned. It wasn't pleasant. "I want Livia to grind her teeth into powder when she sees you on my arm. And then I want us both to smile at her and wish her well after she bows down to you."

"Damn, Max, you should have been a girl. That's totally bitchy."

He picked up one of her hands and kissed the palm, sending more shivers of heat through her. "And then tomorrow we finish moving the rest of your stuff in."

Emma had given in on moving in with him just the night before. She hadn't been to her apartment since the night Max bit her, other than to pick up a few changes of clothing, her toiletries, her full-length mirror that she refused to live without, and her makeup. Her red PT Cruiser had finally made its way to his garage last night, too, and was now nestled next to Max's Durango. He'd frowned darkly over the fact that it was a convertible, muttering something about knives and maniacs, but he'd just have to learn to live with it. Emma loved her car, and her car loved her.

"I'll make you a deal." He'd never go for it, and then she'd get to change costumes. A win-win situation, as far as she was concerned.

"Shoot."

"I'll wear the costume if we take my car to the party."

"Done." Emma's jaw dropped. He hated her car. He'd made it clear he absolutely hated it, but he hadn't even hesitated. He stood, reached out with a finger and shut her mouth. "You're going to be late for work, sweetheart."

"Oh shit!" Emma looked at her watch and bolted for the garage, leaving the costumes behind.

"Emma!"

She turned in the doorway, grabbed the bag he held out with Becky's costume in it and raced out, doing her best to ignore his chuckles. She shoved the bag in the car, opened the garage door and darted back inside.

Max turned, confused as she barreled back into the house at Mach speed. He managed to catch her as she threw herself at him, wrapping her legs around his waist. She pulled his startled face close and kissed him soundly. "Bye!" she yelled as she dropped out of his hold and ran back out the door again, the picture of his stunned, happy face and silly grin staying with her the entire way to work.

"You expect me to wear that?" Becky stared at the costume Emma had laid out on the Victorian sofa in Wallflowers with something akin to horror. "Emma, I thought Max was Zorro. Are you sure you want me to match his costume?"

Emma grinned; Becky was one of the few people who knew about her hook-up with Max. "Max isn't going as Zorro. That was a smokescreen he threw up to keep Livia at bay. Trust me, you won't match Max tonight."

Becky paled as Emma's slight emphasis on Max's name

registered. “Tell me Simon isn’t going as Zorro.”

“Simon isn’t going as Zorro,” Emma deadpanned, already inching her way towards the door.

“Emma!” Becky shrieked, totally horrified.

Emma stopped. “Becky, you’ve been dancing around your attraction for Simon for months, probably years! And you know what? I think he’s just as attracted to you as you are to him! So, why don’t you go for it?”

“You know the type of women Simon goes for! Hell, I know for a fact where he’s been. You think I want to boldly go where everyone else has gone before?”

“Simon hasn’t dated in months, Becks.”

“That’s a lie, Emma. He went out with Belinda just last week!”

“Nope, he didn’t. You have got to stop listening to what those two say, Becky! Trust me, I have inside information. The night Simon was supposed to be with Belinda he was with Max!” Becky looked unconvinced. “Look, let’s try and figure this out logically, okay?”

“Okay,” Becky drawled reluctantly. She seated herself gingerly on the sofa next to the sprawled out Zorro outfit and watched Emma pace.

“Fact one: Livia Patterson is a class-A bitch. Yes or no?”

“Yes.”

“Fact two: Belinda Campbell is also a class-A bitch. Yes or no?”

“Yes.” Becky sighed impatiently.

“Fact three: Livia and Belinda hate our guts for some obscure reason, possibly to do with the fact that cherry punch is a bitch to get out of white satin. Yes or no?”

“Yes.”

"Fact four: Livia and Belinda are both interested in making sure no other woman gets either Max or Simon. Yes or no?"

Becky looked uncomfortable. She bit her lip, suddenly uncertain. "Yes?"

Emma snorted. "Trust me, when Livia finds out I've hooked up with Max she's going to shit a brick." Emma waved off Becky's sputtering, startled laugh with a small frown. "Belinda is just as bad, but she wants Simon."

"So?"

"So, from what I've heard, and seen, I should add, Simon seems to want you."

Becky blinked. "You know, I've heard they've got some pretty good outreach programs for drug abusers. You should look into them."

Emma sighed. "Becky, the man made his Madonna look just like you. Only smiling and happy instead of grouchy. So maybe it doesn't look *exactly* like you."

"Har-de-har-har. Seriously, Emma, Simon's never shown a lick of interest. And, frankly, knowing where his tongue has been I'm not certain I *want* him licking me."

Emma eyed Becky with disgust. "Quit making excuses, Becky. Wear the costume and see how Simon reacts. If he's interested, he'll let you know."

"And if he isn't interested?"

Emma grinned. "Somehow I don't think you need to worry about that." Ignoring Becky's sudden blush, Emma headed out the door. She'd made an appointment to have her hair done for the masquerade and she had no intention of missing it.

The gossip in the salon was running fast and furious. None of the women there knew about her hooking up with Max yet, so a lot of the gossip fluttered around who the town's hottest hunks were taking to the masquerade. Some believed Max was taking Livia, a rumor Livia herself skillfully confirmed without actually confirming anything. Emma had a hard time keeping her snorts of amusement to herself. Max wanted no one to get wind of their relationship until the masquerade when she would enter on his arm; otherwise she would have taken great delight in setting Livia straight. Everyone agreed Simon was the wildcard; no one had any clue who he'd be taking, although Livia tried to make it sound like he'd be taking Belinda. Since Emma knew for a fact that Simon was flying solo, she kept her mouth shut.

Adrian Giordano was also rumored to be flying solo, something Emma could have confirmed but didn't. There were a few other men the women were interested in, but she didn't know those men personally so she just closed her eyes, relaxed into the stylist's chair and let the rumors fly over her head.

"And, of course, we all know Becky will be taking Emma." Emma popped one eye open to see Livia smirking at her. She did the one thing she knew would piss the woman off the most. She smiled serenely and closed her eyes, ignoring her for the rest of her appointment.

Max walked into the house a half an hour late. He had very little time to get showered and dressed before the masquerade, and the quickie he'd been hoping to indulge in wasn't going to happen. The Pride Alpha couldn't be late, especially when he planned on introducing his Curana to the rest of the Pride for the first time.

"Max?"

"Hey, sweetheart." Max put his briefcase down next to the sofa and headed for the bedroom, pulling his tie off as he went.

"How'd your...day...go..."

Emma stood in the middle of the bedroom in the pirate outfit he'd picked out for her. The skirt hit her mid-thigh, just as he'd predicted. The boots hit her just below her knee, showing off an awful lot of skin. The thigh-high stockings were nowhere in evidence, not that she needed them. She'd had her hair styled in a half-up, half-down thing, with curls and twists she normally didn't have, framing her face beautifully. The frilly captain's hat was the icing on the cake.

Her makeup was a little darker and richer than she normally wore. The pale rose lip gloss she preferred had been exchanged for a darker shade, closer to wine. Her eyes were dark and smoky. Thick gold hoops adorned her ears and around her neck was a stylized golden cat. She stood with her hands behind her, an uncertain look on her face, the toe of one boot digging into the carpet as she looked at herself in the full-length mirror she'd moved from her apartment. She looked like a confection just waiting to be eaten. "Max?"

"Huh?" God, he hoped she didn't want him to actually talk, since he was pretty sure he couldn't form complete words, let alone sentences.

She looked at him out of the corner of her eye and bit her lip, and Max nearly swallowed his tongue. "Are you sure this skirt isn't too short?"

Max gulped as he took her in from her incredible face to her edible legs. "Is that a trick question?"

Emma rolled her eyes, some of the uncertainty leeching out of her face as she turned back towards the mirror. "Why don't you go take your shower and get dressed? We have to be at the Friedelinde's in an hour." She reached up to adjust her breasts in her bra and Max nearly fell on the floor. When she shimmied everything back into place, he practically ran for the bathroom.

It was either an ice cold shower or throw her to the ground and mount her, to hell with Jonathon Friedelinde and the masquerade.

He showered quickly, since ice bathing wasn't his favorite sport. He dressed in record time as he listened to Emma putter around the great room muttering to herself. At the last minute he remembered to grab the signet ring before going to gather up Emma.

When he stepped out of the bedroom, he was gratified to see Emma just as spellbound as he'd been when he'd seen her costume. His long jacket was burgundy, with the same gold embroidery that was on her waist cinch and overskirt. Black lace peeked out at his wrists. He wore a black shirt with a black lace jabot underneath, skin-tight black pants and black boots cuffed just below his knees. He carried his saber since he couldn't wear it while driving. His tricorn hat was black with gold trim. Three black feathers in the hat polished off the look.

"Oh boy. If we don't get out of here now, we are so going to be late." Emma's voice was husky with desire and her eyes had turned gold. Max had to struggle not to push her up against the wall, free his aching cock and give them both what they wanted.

Max clenched his hand around the signet ring and stopped, the ring reminding him of something important he had to do before they left. "Wait, give me your hand." Emma held out her right hand. Max took it and gently slipped the signet ring of the Curana onto her middle finger. The Curana's ring was identical to his own, but smaller and daintier. Two stylized pumas surrounded a gold oval, paws to tails. In the center of the oval, the face of a puma had been engraved with two yellow diamonds for eyes. When she looked confused Max held up his own right hand, displaying his ring on his middle finger. "You are my Curana. Now everyone will know it."

Emma stared at the ring on her finger, a slow, utterly content smile stealing across her face.

"Livia is seriously going to shit a brick."

"*Emma!*"

Laughing, she rose up on her toes and kissed him with all the love in her heart, knocking both their hats to the floor in the process.

Chapter Seven

Emma had never seen so many versions of pirate wench and pirate captain in all her life. The wenches ranged from modest, immodest, to downright erotic. One woman actually bragged that her pirate costume was by Playboy! Considering how little there was of it, Emma didn't doubt the woman; compared to her Emma felt as covered as a nun. Then there was the usual assortment of ghosts, vampires, witches and ghouls, with a rare werewolf thrown in for fun. Jamie and Marie Howard had both come as gunslingers in matching black outfits and cowboy hats, both looking happy and proud enough to burst over the success of their party. They were the first to notice the ring on Emma's hand, and, with warm smiles and friendly hugs, they congratulated her and Max on their mating.

As Max and Emma moved through the crowd, other people came to congratulate them. Jonathon Friedelinde was polite, if somewhat cool. It irritated Max, but Emma understood on some level that Mr. Friedelinde was taking a "wait and see" attitude. In fact, Jonathon's attitude was the one that prevailed among the men as more and more people became aware of Max's mating. Everyone had expected him to pick someone as strong as he was, and none of them truly believed Emma was strong enough. The women, on the other hand, were, well, cattier. By the time they found Adrian, Max was trembling with the need to force his will on all of his Pride and *make* them accept his mate, something that would diminish Emma further in their eyes. Hell, she might be new to this whole Puma gig, but she knew this was one battle Max couldn't fight for her.

"Hey, Adrian." Emma smiled wearily. By the end of the first hour, she'd become so busy holding Max back that she didn't have time to worry about her outfit.

"Hey, Emma. Congratulations." Adrian dipped his head to her with a warm smile, shocking her. She'd had no idea Adrian was one of them.

Max nodded back, and Emma followed suit. "Thanks, Adrian. Have you seen Simon yet?"

"Oh, you mean Zorro?" Adrian grinned, gesturing with his hand. "He's over there, trying to chase down this cute little bandita."

"Becky's here?" Emma craned her neck and went on tip-toes, but it was no use; she was just too damn short to see over anybody. With a huff, she settled back down and glared at Max, waiting.

"Would you like to go see Becky now?" Max asked, smirking. He was staring off to his left, tracking someone through the crowd.

"Frigging tall people," she muttered, trying to see past the crowd of bodies to where Max was looking.

She squealed with surprise when Max bent down and picked her up, practically sitting her on his shoulder. She daintily crossed her ankles and held on for dear life as she scanned the crowd. "There! She's heading into the garden. Aw, son of a bitch."

"What?" Max asked, holding her steady with little effort.

"Simon's just been waylaid by Belinda. By the way, she *so* picked the right costume."

"Witch?"

"Catwoman. From the movie."

"Ah, sexy yet lame." Max winced when Emma tweaked his ear. "I'll rescue Simon, you find Becky." He set her down gently, careful to make sure her skirt didn't fly up, up and away. With a quick kiss and a nod at Adrian, Max went after Simon.

Emma found moving through the crowd without Max at her side more difficult. It seemed like people went out of their way to get in her way. "Excuse me, pardon me, excuse me." Emma tried to be polite as she shimmied around more than one person. When she reached a particularly large knot of people, she tried the polite route, though by this time she was becoming seriously irritated. She tapped the broad shoulder of a vampire standing in front of her. "Excuse me, let me pass, please."

The vampire ignored her, laughing with his companions.

"Excuse me, please, I need to get into the garden."

The vampire continued to ignore her.

"Will you please excuse me?" Emma practically shouted.

The vampire turned, frowned down at her, and turned back to his companions with a shrug and a laugh.

Emma lost it. Her temper, frayed by the tension in Max and the subtle snubs to herself, snapped. Emma could feel a strange power flowing through her, tied to yet separate from the Puma, and without thought she used it.

Her eyes narrowed on the group in front of her. The tone of command was the same one Max had used on her several times, the same one she was able to (almost) ignore. Power flowed out of her, surrounding her till she nearly glowed with it.

"Move out of my way."

The crowd behind them grew quiet as the men stopped

laughing. The men in front of her visibly cringed and got out of her way, their heads bowing down, their shoulders hunching against Emma's anger. Using her power like the prow of a ship, Emma forged her way through the rest of the crowd, her head held high as she stepped into the garden.

With a deep breath, Emma sucked that power back into her body. It settled in, warm and cozy, purring but ready to pounce. The Puma, she sensed, was pleased with her display of dominance.

The garden was well lit, except in strategically placed spots where pools of darkness prevailed. Emma was pretty sure what went on in those spots, and hoped her nose would help her keep out of other people's business. Sniffing cautiously, she tried to scent Becky.

The sharp tang of coppery blood filled her senses, mixed with Becky's earthy scent. Emma stepped into the garden and made a beeline for the smell. Halfway there, she heard Becky scream.

Emma began to run.

Max finally pried Belinda off Simon by ordering her off. With a coy shrug, the woman finally let go, but not before giving both men a peek at what they were walking away from.

"Ugh." Simon shuddered. "You'd think she'd get the hint. 'Get off me, get off me, what the hell are you doing, get off me' just didn't seem to get through to her."

Max snickered. Simon was brushing at his shirt as if he could brush Belinda's scent off of him. "Becky seems to have headed into the garden. Emma went to find her."

"In this crowd?" Simon stopped brushing himself and straightened his hat. "I heard a couple of the young bloods claim they were going to 'test' Emma."

Max growled. "How?"

"The usual. Forcing her to use her powers. She's small enough that simply not getting out of her way will do it."

Max's smile was feral. "In that case, they're in for a surprise."

"Never doubted it."

The two men waited until they felt the burst of power flowing from a point not far from the garden doors. It was strong enough to nearly have Max bowing down before it. Simon actually grimaced before pulling himself upright by force of will alone. Emma had finally gotten fed up and was forcing her way through the crowd, her strength clearly a match for, if not slightly greater than, Max's. Max and Simon managed to find spots where they could watch her regal exit from the ballroom. Her head moved neither left nor right; her eyes were pure molten gold. She flowed towards the garden doors, her stride sleek and sultry, commanding the attention of all around her. There was more than one shocked face in the crowd as Emma, her power swirling around her like a cape, stepped out of the double doors and into the Friedelinde's garden, every inch the Curana Max had claimed her to be.

"My God, she is so fucking hot." Max grinned as he watched his pissed-off mate saunter out into the night, the sexy sway of her hips riveting to more than one pair of male eyes. He was unsurprised at how the Pumas around her practically scraped the floor in her wake.

"Yeah. Good for you. Go home soon, fuck like bunnies, make little Alphas for Uncle Simon and Aunt Becky to play with. Speaking of which, can we go get *my* woman now?" Simon grumbled, already beginning to push through the crowd.

Max merely grinned, too pleased with and proud of Emma to call Simon to task. He moved through the crowd on Simon's heels, almost barreling into him when the man stopped. "Simon?"

Simon looked over his shoulder at Max, confusion and fear mingling in his expression. "I smell blood."

Max sniffed. There, on the evening breeze, was the tang of blood mixed with Becky, Emma...and Livia?

Simon's eyes went gold as his claws ripped through the leather swordsman's gloves. "Becky's bleeding." He took off into the night, following the blood trail of his mate.

"Fuck." Max chased after his friend, knowing that if Livia had hurt Becky it would take a miracle to keep Simon from killing her.

Emma took in the scene before her, trying not to shudder. Livia had Becky pinned beneath her, her claws going for Becky's soft stomach, her teeth at Becky's throat. Becky stared at Emma, obviously terrified, bleeding from numerous small cuts inflicted by Livia's claws, and one bad-looking bite wound on her left shoulder. Her unsheathed sword was just beyond her reach, probably knocked out of her hand when Livia pounced. Her hat had fallen off during the scuffle as well, landing brim up next to a rosebush. Livia had cuts on her arms and a slash in her right cheek, showing Becky had fought back.

Livia snarled, the warning of one cat to another over prey, and Becky froze.

Emma cocked her hip, hands going to her waist as she tried to still the frantic beating of her heart. She had to hit Livia where she lived, get her to turn on *her* and get the hell off of Becky before someone died. "Okay, some of the peroxide must have leaked into your brains to make *this* seem like a good idea. What will killing Becky accomplish, other than to piss off Simon and Max *and* ruin your manicure?" Livia snarled again, but she didn't tighten her hold on Becky's throat. Her claws remained poised above Becky's stomach. Emma racked her brains, trying to think of ways to get Livia's undivided attention. "Did you run out of Liversnaps or something? Oh wait, that's dogs."

Livia dug her claws into Becky's stomach, making her gasp. Red beads of blood, black in the night, dribbled down Becky's sides as Livia released her throat and sat up slowly. Her hand flexed, driving her claws in deeper. "I want the Curana's ring."

Emma stared at her, stunned. "A ring does not make you Curana, Livia."

Livia sneered. "It does to them!" She tossed her head towards the house, indicating all the other Pumas inside. "If they see I took the ring from you, they'll never acknowledge you as Curana." She smiled, her fangs glistening in the moonlight. "They'll see you for the weak, pathetic wallflower you've always been. Max will be mine, like he always should have been; he won't have a choice. He and I will run the Pride the way it was meant to be run, and you'll be seen as nothing but the Alpha's whore."

Emma nodded thoughtfully. It took everything she had to stay focused on Livia and not her friend. "Yeah, all of that is true. Except for one thing. Well, two, really."

"What's that?"

"One, Max doesn't want your double-processed skanky ass."

"Hey! I'm a natural blonde!"

The woman is obviously a few tacos short of a fiesta platter. Emma mentally rolled her eyes. She was so done dealing with Livia. "Two, even without the ring, I *am* the Curana." Emma's power punched out, reaching for the woman in front of her. "Let Becky go. Now."

Livia whimpered as Emma forced her to do her bidding. Her

hand trembled with the force of Emma's command, her claws slowly, reluctantly withdrawing from Becky's stomach. She crawled on all fours off of Becky, her shoulders hunched. Emma's will compelled her away from the bleeding woman.

"Kneel."

Emma's command punched out, forcing Livia to her knees. She shook with the need to break free, her breath panting in and out of laboring lungs, but Emma kept her tied to her will.

Out of the corner of her eye, Emma saw Max helping Becky, which left her free to deal with Livia. Or so she thought.

The sound she heard behind her caused the hair on the back of her neck to stand on end. She now knew why pumas had earned the nickname mountain screamer as Simon's Puma let loose a high-pitched yowl at the sight of his injured mate. Before Emma could stop him, Simon pounced on Livia, claws extended, and bore her to the ground.

"I should kill you where you lay," he snarled over her, digging his claws into her stomach in the same exact spot she'd wounded Becky. The scent of blood and fear were thick in the air as Simon leaned down, his canines extending. "I could rip your throat out right now."

Emma glanced over at Becky and saw her shuddering in fear, held in place only by Max's arms. "Uh, Simon?" Golden eyes blinded by rage met hers. "You're scaring the crap out of Becky."

She watched as he looked over at Becky. The sight of her seemed to calm him somewhat, though his claws never left Livia's flesh.

"Becky." Becky jumped at the sound of his voice, moaning as her wounds bled some more. "What would you have me do to her?"

Max's gasp was audible; in essence, Simon was giving

Becky the kill.

"Simon?" It was more of a plea than a question, but for what Emma didn't know.

"Tell me, Becky. What should Livia's punishment be for injuring you?"

Becky blinked back tears and stared at Livia. "What is she? What are you?"

"Pumas. Werecats. I'll explain more later. Right now, you need to decide her punishment."

Becky looked at Emma, who cringed to see the confusion and hurt on her best friend's face. "I didn't know until Max bit me, then I didn't know if you would believe me or not. But I planned on telling you tomorrow, if Simon didn't do it first."

"You're a..." Becky swallowed hard at Emma's slow nod. "And they're..." Emma watched as Becky absorbed the information. When she blew out a hard breath, Emma relaxed. "This is going to cost you a fortune in Tidy Cat." Becky's laugh was shaky but Emma knew everything would be all right.

Emma grinned. "What would you like Simon to do with Livia?"

"What can he do with Livia?" Becky asked, staring down at Livia.

"Well, let's see: she was willing to kill you to get the Curana's ring, so Simon is well within his rights to rip out her throat." Emma shrugged. "Wouldn't be all that big a loss as far as I'm concerned."

"What the hell is the Curana's ring?"

"It's the ring Emma now wears that proclaims she's my mate and queen," Max replied, gentling his grip on Becky's arms as he realized she was reacting to the news far better than he'd expected.

"Whoa. Wait, so I was bait for Emma?"

"Becky, the longer Simon smells the blood, the harder it will be for him to not kill Livia. Decide her fate quickly."

Becky looked at Livia one last time before staring straight into Simon's golden eyes. "What is the lowest status a Puma can hold? If Max is king and Emma is queen, is there a lowest of the low?"

"No!" Livia moaned, trying to break free of Simon's hold. Simon merely dug his claws in deeper while his other hand held her down by her throat.

"Outcast," he answered. "Someone who's been made Prideless. She'll hold no privileges, no responsibilities. She will no longer be welcome at Pride functions or homes. Kits will be taught to avoid her. If she wished for status again she would have to leave, find a Pride willing to take her in and earn it."

Becky nodded. "Since the whole damn thing was about status, I think that would do nicely."

Simon nodded with a slow smile of approval. He bowed his head formally to Max. "My mate requests a casting out of the one named Olivia Patterson." He ignored Becky's startled gasp and Livia's moaned denial.

Max eased Becky gently to the ground before stepping up beside Emma. He positioned himself so that Becky could see everything that was happening between them. His right hand, the one with the Alpha's ring, came to rest on Emma's hip as he stared down at Livia. "The Beta of this Pride has requested a formal casting out. My Curana witnessed the unprovoked attack of our Beta's mate, Rebecca Yaeger." Emma saw Becky shoot Simon a narrow-eyed glare. "The attack was motivated by greed rather than self-defense. In light of these allegations I ask you, Olivia Patterson: how do you plead?"

"Fuck you." Livia tried once more to buck off Simon, but he

didn't budge an inch. Emma hoped she was having trouble breathing with the massive artist sitting on her chest.

Max's expression turned icy cold as he stared at the woman who'd tried to hurt Becky and steal his mate's power. "I'll take that as a guilty." Max's power whispered forth, like a slow moving mist, creeping out onto the grounds and into the house. As that fog of power touched the Pumas, they became aware of what was happening in the garden, if not exactly why. "As Alpha of this Pride, for the unprovoked attack against the Beta's mate, I hereby declare Olivia Patterson outcast. You are no longer one of us. You may no longer run with us, or hunt with us. You are no longer welcome in our homes. You may no longer approach our kits without risk to your life."

Livia began to sob quietly as Max formally kicked her out of the Pride. "Any attack on you will go unpunished within the Pride; we leave you to human laws. If you attack a mate of one of ours, you will be dealt with as an outsider, and your life will be forfeit. Any further contact with Rebecca Yaeger will be considered an attack, and will be dealt with as such. Again, your life will be forfeit. Any Pride member giving you succor will suffer the same fate as you." With a gentle nudge, Max turned so that he and Emma had their backs to Livia, effectively dismissing her. Simon pulled his claws from her flesh, his eyes returning to their normal dark brown, his fangs receding as he approached Becky.

"Um, down, kitty? Good kitty?" Becky smiled weakly as Simon reached for her. Simon gently picked Becky up, careful of her wounds, and walked out of the garden, undoubtedly headed for the cars parked in front of the Friedelinde's mansion. A long overdue conversation was about to take place, and if Emma wasn't wrong some more biting was also going to take place.

"Will Simon's bite heal Becky's wounds?" Emma asked as

they slowly walked away from the weeping woman huddled on the ground behind them.

"For the most part. She'll bear some scars, most likely on her neck where Livia bit her, but otherwise she'll be fine. I'm pretty sure Simon will take care of that quickly."

"Hmm. What do you think Livia will do?" Emma tucked her hand in the crook of Max's arm and leaned on him. Her feet were beginning to hurt in the damn boots he'd bought her.

"Move, preferably far, far away." Max picked up Emma's hand and kissed the back of her knuckles. "You, by the way, were magnificent, my Curana."

Emma grinned up at him. "You think so?"

"I saw your performance in the house, and part of it out here." Max stopped and pulled her into his arms, his mouth brushing against his mark on her neck. "Watching you put all those assholes in their place really got me hot."

Emma giggled and wriggled her hips against him. "I thought I rocked."

Max purred slightly as he nipped the mark on her neck. "Simon told me I should take you home and start making kits. What do you think?" Max looked down at her, love and lust glowing equally in his brilliant smile.

She leaned into him as they began walking back to the house, Livia forgotten behind them. Her hand rubbed his chest absently, her ring gleaming in the moonlight. "Max?"

"What?" His tone was wary; he'd come to expect the unexpected when she used that particular tone of voice.

"Will I give birth to a baby or a litter?"

"Emma," he groaned.

"I mean, will we be feeding them baby formula or Kitten Chow?"

"Emma!"

"If they get stuck in a tree, who do we call? Does the fire department *do* kitten rescues anymore? This is important stuff to know, Lion-O!"

"God save me." She could tell from the way his chest rumbled under her hand that he was holding back a laugh.

"Too late. Oh, and we're not naming any kids Richard. I mean, Dick Cannon? Almost as bad as Max Cannon. Has anyone ever mentioned you have a name like a porn star? I mean, not that you don't have the equipment to live up to it."

"Emma!"

Emma giggled.

Life was good.

About the Author

Dana Marie Bell wrote her first short story when she was thirteen years old. She attended the High School for Creative and Performing Arts for creative writing, where freedom of expression was the order of the day. When her parents moved out of the city and placed her in a Catholic high school for her senior year she tried desperately to get away, but the nuns held fast, and she graduated with honors despite herself.

Dana has lived primarily in the Northeast (Pennsylvania, New Jersey and Delaware, to be precise), with a brief stint on the US Virgin Island of St. Croix. She lives with her soul-mate and husband Dusty, their two maniacal children, two evil ice-cream stealing cats, and a bull terrier that thinks it's a Pekinese.

You can learn more about Dana at: www.danamariebell.com.

Look for these titles by

Dana Marie Bell

Now Available:

Sweet Dreams

Cat of a Different Color

Very Much Alive

Coming Soon:

Dare to Believe

Treasure Hunting

J. B. McDonald

Dedication

For my parents, who never blinked when I said I was going to be a writer, and who proudly announced the publication of my romance to their church group.

And for Sabina, who pitched in at the last minute and kept me from hysterics.

Chapter One

The only problem with South America—aside from giant bugs, a lack of air conditioning, and general chauvinism—was that you could walk right past an ancient ruin and never know it.

Meg had no intention of doing so, but that was easier said than done. Still, she supposed it made her travel guides happy—they were able to set up camp and remain there while she quartered the surrounding jungle one foot at a time. What she really needed, she thought as she whacked through a hanging branch and cleared six more inches, was Tarzan. Yes, Tarzan would be the perfect trail guide. And maybe, just maybe, he'd know a shortcut to any possible rui—

She stopped, having caught a glimpse of...*something* out of the corner of her eye. Her feet squished in the soft ground as she leaned back. An insect bit her, and she slapped at it absently.

There. Between the trees.

Heart pounding, she turned and began the mad scramble to get through the underbrush. It could have been stone. It also could have been a funny slant of light coming through the jungle canopy. Most times, it was just light, but maybe *this* time...

Hope sprung eternal, after all. Sweat dripping down her

back and between her breasts, her shirt plastered to her body and various cuts and scrapes adorning her arms, she finally forced her way through.

It was just a slant of light.

Meg sighed heavily and sat, checking to make sure there was a root rather than slime to sit on. She glared at a mosquito, then squished it when it had the audacity to try and bite her.

Three more weeks. Three more weeks of leave, and then she had to go back to being a staid college professor. Back to grading papers and helping students through academic crises, trying to convince them that sociology was great. She'd have to give up treasure hunting for a while longer, until the next major break—Christmas. She thought she might be able to wrangle it free without getting a *complete* guilt trip from her mother. Just a partial guilt trip. Okay, slightly more than "partial". But it would be worth it, to be able to gather up her savings (frivolously spent, if her father was asked) and hare back down here to South America, braving theft and soldiers and giant bugs from outer space.

She brushed some kind of uber-large beetle away and glowered.

Damn it.

She peered into the heavy green jungle overhead, trying to gauge how much light was left. Probably enough for another half hour of hacking and slicing before she had to hack and slice her way back to camp. She pushed back to her feet, rubbing sweat away with a dirty wrist, and started off again.

Another fifteen minutes flew by, another few feet were gained. Birds screamed above and animals watched her pass. The jungle was loud in a way the city never could be, filled with animals and bugs and the rustle of leaves against vines, against branches, against bark. Noises that faded into the background until a monkey screeched or a bird exploded out of nearby foliage, and eventually even those became less noticeable.

Gunfire shattered the noise. In the hair-lifting quiet that echoed afterward, her breath shuddered in her throat.

Her head whipped around, feet nearly catching in the mud and sending her sprawling. Visions of armed men attacking their camp snarled through her mind, and she felt for the rifle her guides had insisted she take. She raced back toward their base, discarding initial attempts to do so quietly. There was no chance of that happening.

She was halfway there when a shape darting from one shadow to the next sent her slamming against a tree trunk, trying to hide. A heartbeat passed before she realized that whatever that was, it wasn't human. Nobody moved with such silence through the heavy jungle, no matter how long they'd lived there. She slid out from her cover, watching for the creature.

Men shouted, but there were no more shots. Even the yelling didn't seem frantic—excited, maybe, but not panicked. Not an attack, then? An animal? She moved closer to where the thing had crossed her path, gaze casting through the humid greenery in search of—well, she wasn't sure, but in search of something.

A smear of blood caught her eye. She hesitated, logic telling her that whatever they'd shot would likely be dead in a matter of minutes. Probably an animal, probably not a person—or if it was a person, an armed and angry one.

Despite all of the reasons to leave it alone, she found herself following the thin trail the creature had left. The occasional broken twig—and how anything moved through this forest leaving it so untouched was a wonder—added to the occasional bloody stripe across leaves, marking its path. When she found a paw print as big as her fist, she nearly stopped the search. Her guides were going to throw a fit if she brought an animal back that they'd just shot. But, damn it, at the very least she had to make sure it wasn't suffering.

Meg pushed on. All things considered, it wasn't long before she stumbled across—

A tail.

She blinked.

A really long tail. Shadow-dark, with ebony rosettes and a lethally black tip. This was no little critter needing help. This was large, a predator that could eat her in a single bite. Maybe even half a bite. She really wasn't that big.

Cautiously, she pushed aside fronds to see the rest of the animal.

Jaguar, her mind whispered in equal parts awe and terror.

The cat lay coiled, a foreleg hanging almost uselessly to one side. Tawny gold eyes regarded her without blinking, ears flat back against its head. Sleek fur stretched, graceful over impossibly perfect muscles. Claws flexed into the dirt, either in threat or preparation to flee—she couldn't tell. It wouldn't get much farther on that leg, though. Blood matted the fur, a furrow cutting straight through the powerful shoulder.

Pausing, she unslung her rifle and aimed carefully through the sights. Her heart sank, staring into gold eyes that glared defiantly back at her. It was going to die—slowly and painfully, if left to the mercy of infection and other animals. What she was doing was a blessing. Really.

Her finger just wouldn't tighten on the trigger.

She cursed and lowered her rifle. With hurried, frustrated movements—what she was doing was insane, and she wasn't sure she could convince her guides to help—she slung the rifle back over her shoulder and pulled out the tranquilizer gun. She'd *told* the guides to use them in case of an animal attack, but obviously they hadn't listened.

She could do it, though, and she could *make* them listen. The jaguar would have to be enough treasure for this trip—hell, rescuing a predator ought to at least make for several years' worth of stories, right? Right, she decided, then lifted her gun and shot.

The jaguar screamed, the jungle incarnate. Then it relaxed, eyelids drooping closed as its eyes rolled back in their sockets.

Perfect. Now to lug several hundred pounds of flesh and muscle back to the camp.

Maybe she should have thought this through a little more.

It took the promise of an extra fifty American dollars per person to get her three guides to help. They bound the big cat, tying all four feet together, and then hefted it back to their base. Night had fallen by the time the cat was secured to a downed tree, rope tight enough to reassure the men that it wasn't going to break free and attack. From the looks they were shooting her, Meg guessed they would be just as happy to tie her up and make sure there wouldn't be any other surprise pets.

She spent several minutes feeling around the cat's legs, looking for a pulse before finally giving up and trusting that the tranquilizer makers knew what they were doing. Then she pulled out the heavy-duty first aid kit she always brought along and prepared to clean the wound. After a moment's thought on how to avoid claws should the cat wake up and take offense to her help, she positioned herself behind its shoulder.

It didn't wake, though, and only twitched when she flushed the injury with alcohol.

It wasn't bleeding badly. She stuffed the bullet graze full of gauze and taped the padding to the creature's fur before finishing for the night. After checking the ropes and making certain they were neither too tight nor too loose—she might feel bad for the big predator, but she wasn't about to become its next meal—Meg crawled into her tent of bug mesh and curled up to sleep.

ꟈ

An engine started. Meg grabbed for her pillow to pull it over her head, determined that the L.A. traffic wouldn't wake her.

She couldn't find her pillow.

Then she remembered she wasn't in L.A.

Curly blonde hair fell in tangles before her face as she jerked awake. Blowing it out of the way impatiently, she scrambled free of mosquito netting and staggered into the jungle.

By jarring beams of flashlights her guides threw the last of their belongings into a Jeep that idled fifty feet away, on the dirt path they called a road.

"What are you doing?" Meg yelled, stumbling into the strip of jungle separating their camp from the cars. Her foot squelched in something slimy, her hand smashing into a tree in her attempt to keep from falling. She stopped moving, half afraid of running into something *else* in her dash forward.

Then a body brushed by, and she grabbed at a bulky wrist. Peering up, she realized she'd caught her head guide. "We've got another three weeks!"

"Sorry, *señora*." He pulled free and shouldered the bag she'd knocked loose. "We've left one Jeep for you, to come back when you will. The men—they do not like *El Gato*."

"The cat? This is about my *jaguar*?" she asked disbelievingly. "It's trussed up!"

"Sorry, *señora*." Juan shrugged once and tossed his bag to a man already sitting in the back of the auto. "You will be fine. Don't worry. No one will bother him." He yanked a thumb back toward their camp and the tied jaguar. Then he vaulted into the Jeep.

"Juan! Damn it!" Meg shouted, tripping on God-knew-what in the dark and cursing violently as the men peeled away.

She stood on the dirt path, glaring down it as taillights flickered and were lost in the foliage. Apparently, good help was hard to find wherever you were.

Muttering under her breath, she staggered back toward the camp. Eventually, she saw the glow of the banked fire, and, relieved that the dark was broken, she headed toward it. All this, for a stupid jaguar. Maybe she should have just shot it. Meg squinted into the blackness where the cat slept.

There didn't seem to be a cat there. In fact, it looked like one of the men had stayed behind after all.

"Fuck," she growled, indulging in the word her mother hated the most. She stomped to the shadowy figure, drawing back to kick it in the thigh and wake it up—

And stopped.

A pristine white bandage was taped to the back of the man's shoulder. A well-muscled, bare shoulder. If any of her guides had possessed shoulders like that, she would have spent a lot less time in the forest.

The shoulder led to a gold-skinned arm. A bare chest rose and fell, breathing with a rhythm just slower than resting. Muscles rippled across chest and stomach, shadows filling hollows with soft darkness. The stomach led to narrow hips and—

Whoa. He was really naked.

Meg swallowed and dragged her gaze back up, uncertain whether she was grateful or upset that his knees, tucked up against his stomach due to his ankles bound up with his hands, hid the rest of him.

No, on second thought, she was definitely upset. She valiantly kept her eyes at a higher point anyway—a relatively easy task, since she couldn't see anything interesting without straddling the man. Maybe if she leaned around—no, no. She forced herself straight again.

He had black hair and thick, dark lashes lying against high cheekbones. A strong jaw created the slightest of hollows in his cheeks, full lips relaxed in sleep. He was stunning—and a great deal more muscled than the men in her group had been.

Cautiously, she inched closer and peeled up the edge of the medical tape, wincing when a layer of skin went with it.

There was a furrow along the shoulder blade, digging into flesh and muscle, looking something like a bullet wound. She glanced around. No sign of the cat. No drag marks. Getting a body that big through this much jungle couldn't have been done without any sign of passing, and yet...

Yet there was no cat, just a very large, very attractive man bound where a jaguar used to be.

This, Meg decided, had to be the South American version of "fool the tourist". She went back to bed.

Angry cat noises woke her. A tabby owned Meg, and she was overly familiar with those noises. Usually, it meant imminent destruction of furniture. When the cat weighed better than three hundred pounds...

She bolted out of her tent, scrambling to her feet amidst tangles of mosquito netting and mud.

The jaguar was right back where it had been the night before, struggling against ties and screaming catty insults at her. She knew catty insults when she heard them.

Rope began to fray.

With a yelp, she grabbed for the tranquilizer gun, loading a shot and plugging the creature as quickly as she could. After one last flail, it dropped unconscious.

Hand to her chest to keep her pounding heart inside, Meg stood and stared at the jaguar. Her mind whirled. Why the men hadn't woken her before the cat freaked out, she couldn't—

Then she remembered the night before. A dream. It had to have been a dream. A close inspection of the camp and what was left—or rather, how much was missing—suggested otherwise.

All right, so a partial dream. Funny light and shadows playing with her vision, combining with entirely too much celibacy, making her think she was seeing a person. Because that—she peered at the jaguar—while beautiful, was no human.

She glared around the camp, then finally dug out rations—the men had left everything she might need, including food and extra bullets—and ate breakfast. By the time she'd finished and cleaned up, she'd convinced herself this really was some asshole attempt at "scare the tourist", and decided to play along. She changed the bandage on the cat, then gathered her things and headed out—only to circle back and lie in wait.

"I'll catch them this time," Meg grumbled to herself, falling back into old habits, "and show them they can't scare me so easily. Assholes." She grinned. She had male cousins—swapping a jaguar with a man and back again wouldn't chase her off.

The day dragged on, heat building under the low canopy. Bugs buzzed, hummed, chirped and crawled. Birds hooted and shrieked and whistled. Small animals crept, climbed and dashed.

She waited and wished something would happen.

At first, she didn't realize what she was seeing. The jaguar seemed changed every time she looked over—legs longer, tail shorter, shoulders broadening. She brushed it off as a trick of the light, fatigue twisting her vision, sheer boredom.

But it kept changing.

Meg stared as the transformation continued, fur seeming to melt into the shadows and disappear, leaving behind golden skin. Black hair lay in his face, obscuring strong features, but the body was unmistakable.

It was the same man she'd seen the night before. No one had moved him.

"Oh," she breathed. "Oh, *shit.*"

Chapter Two

Meg had long since crept out of her hiding place and taken up watch roughly six inches from the man's face. In the light of day shadow and knees couldn't entirely hide the rest of him, and she couldn't help but sneak a peek.

He looked nice. Or maybe, as her younger sister would say, niiiiiiiiiice.

Of course, the fact that he was, apparently, some bizarre kind of cat-man made it unsettling. Still, no sign of fur, no tail, no penis spurs—she double-checked those last two items in the interest of *science*, of course—no claws, the ears were normally rounded, the shoulders were utterly drool-worthy—

It was a battle to keep her mind out of the gutter. Really.

Eventually, though, she'd exhausted her search for signs of the jaguar he'd been and realized that this looked like a normal human. So, she sat six inches from him and watched, mind whirling.

"The Aztec believed that—" Meg paused, the name escaping her. "They had a god that changed into a cat, or something like that," she said to no one in particular. "And the Olmec and Mayan had similar beliefs."

The cat-man slept on, apparently uncaring about the Mayan and Aztec, much less the Olmec.

She couldn't bring herself to voice the rest of the thought—that maybe they'd been right. On the other hand, she thought as she eyed the long body, he did have a rather god-like physique.

Afternoon was well on its way when long, blunt fingers began to twitch. Another fifteen minutes passed as Meg ticked her fingers along the dirt. She organized leaves into piles and dug tiny trenches with nearby sticks, before heavily lashed eyelids did something like fluttering, only a whole lot more masculine. Eyes opened to slits, green-gold irises peering through, pupils dilating and contracting rapidly.

She bent to meet his gaze. "Hi."

The man jerked, yanking at his bound arms and legs as if preparing to run. His face paled. Blood soaked through the white bandage.

"Oh, hell." She scrambled for the first aid kit. The contents spilled across the ground when she snapped it open, and she pawed through things without putting them back. Gathering more gauze, medical tape, and the tube of antibiotic ointment, she turned back. The god-cat-man was eyeing her, still pinned on his side, fingers working at the knots of rope around his ankles.

For a moment, she nearly bent down and untied him herself. Then she saw the forest in his eyes, and remembered the rage of the jaguar—a jaguar with rather large teeth, and even larger claws. And she didn't mean that euphemistically.

"Just—stay still." She inched closer.

He pulled away, but couldn't get far with his arms and legs restrained. Meg, wary of white canines bared by full lips, reached across his shoulder and peeled away the soiled bandage. When he didn't move, she grew a little more confident, pulling off old gauze and tossing it aside. He began to settle, and she uncapped the tube of goo, squeezed some out, then dabbed it over the bullet wound, marveling at golden skin stretched across planes of hard muscle. He was lean, angular, all bronzed. When the cream had stopped the bleeding, she put another gauze pad on top of the wound and taped it carefully, smoothing her fingers over his shoulder blade and down across the indent of his spine.

He didn't seem to object. Tentatively, unable to believe he was actually a real person—what with him having been a real jaguar and all just recently—Meg trailed her fingers down his torso, pausing at long scars. Four in a row, and it struck her that they were claw marks arcing over human flesh. With gentle strokes, she began to trace them. He twitched his shoulders, rolling to bring her back in sight, moving so fast that believing he was some strange were-cat wasn't such a stretch of the imagination.

Gold eyes bored into her, as if willing her to understand something.

"I suppose it's too much that you might speak English?" she sighed.

A heavy black brow rose sardonically, as if—while he might not understand the words—he got the gist of it.

"*Habla español?*" She couldn't think of a single reason *why* the Aztec-Olmec-were-cat-god-man might speak the local tongue. She really hoped he didn't speak Aztec. That could get problematic.

He hesitated, then in Spanish returned, "Where am I?"

She resisted the urge to call "Hallelujah", but couldn't quite stop the grin that spread across her face. "Our camp," she answered, in her own badly accented version of the language. "You were hurt."

His next words were sharp, green-gold eyes turning gold

and black, hard as agate. Meg hadn't been able to catch the entire sentence, but the tone was accusation.

"Not me, my friend," she said in English, smiling and shaking her head. She couldn't seem to stop the smile. Hell, after finding a minor deity trussed up in her camp, she didn't think she should have to. *Come to South America*, the brochures should read, *capture your own sun god!*

His suspicious look didn't dissipate.

"I'm sorry." She switched back to Spanish. "I didn't—" Uncertain of the word for shoot, she paused. "Blaze at you."

Agate eyes softened with complete and total confusion.

"Point at you?" she tried.

He stared at her.

"Throw metal at you?"

He blinked twice, cat-like, then sighed and laid down on the soft ground. She had the sudden urge to rub his belly.

"Friends?" It seemed silly to keep him tied up, but she found herself intimidated of the jaguar he had been.

Jaguar he had been? She was losing her ever lovin' mind. Too much South American research. Next she'd be dreaming of finding the legendary city of gold. Wait, no, even that would make more sense.

He slanted a look at her, thick lashes giving an eye-tilted, feline impression. "Friends," he agreed tentatively.

Meg nodded once, then proceeded to untie the knots. She chuckled when she saw them. He'd just about managed to free himself.

Loose, he stretched and rose, one foot braced on the forest loam, the other crossed. It gave him a tiny semblance of modesty.

Pity.

Pulling her mind out of the gutter she stood, trying to drag her focus away from the wounded man. She strode to her tent, shaking free a light blanket and carrying it back. “Here.” She handed it to him selflessly. How many other sex-starved women would help a minor deity cover up? Not many, she’d bet.

He reached out right-handed, then flinched and dropped his arm when his shoulder pulled. Face pale, he reached out with his left hand and let the blanket pool in his lap, his expression tight with pain. “Thank you.” The words were soft, a purr deep in a well-muscled chest.

Her mouth went dry. “Ohhhh, boy,” she murmured, rubbing her stomach. *Something* needed to be touching her. “Ohhhh, boy, oh boy, oh boy.”

He stared at her, eyes slowly going darker, turning the more common brown that was seen so often in this region.

“Oh boy,” Meg said one more time, feeling heat pool in her muscles and spread out, tingling to her fingertips. “Too sexual,” her last boyfriend had told her, explaining that he was rising in the world and her blatant need for sex would hamper him. She was too much of a wild child, cavorting around and spouting nonsense theories on hidden ruins and treasure hunting. It hadn’t been the first time she’d been accused of such things, but—hellllllll. How could you *not* be sexual when confronted with *El Gato*, the perfect image of an Aztec god?

He was inspecting her again, a slow, knowing smile spreading over full lips. The expression reached clear up to now-black eyes. Ebony hair hung just past his shoulders, straight and silky and begging to be petted. She realized she was reaching toward him about the same time he tipped his head and kissed the palm of her hand, tongue flicking out to brush against skin.

She jumped back, feeling as though she might have been

burned. "Ahh—holy crap, you're a crazy god-man who turns into a freakin' *cat*!" she nearly yelled, resisting the urge to hug herself just for the touch. "I'm losing my mind!"

His gaze remained on her, lust washed away by bemusement.

"Oh, God, I don't know what I'm going to *do* with you!" Meg spoke English and didn't care, babbling away in her own personal freak-out. She figured that after being abandoned in the jungle with a mythical creature, she deserved it. In fact, it was probably long overdue.

"I know what I'm going to do," she announced, scratching fingernails through her short hair as she tromped to her tent. "I'm going to go find that little bathing pool and take a damn bath. Not a cold bath, mind you," she babbled, "because nothing in this damn country is cold, but it'll at least be lukewarm instead of *this* hot." Because what she felt could only be classified as hot, really. She grabbed a dirty shirt—well, dirtier than the others—to use as a towel and whipped around, looking at the cat-man. "Don't move," she ordered, switching back to Spanish.

He inclined his head, letting hair spill over his shoulders in a wave of shadow. "Of course," he answered in kind.

Meg stared at him for a moment longer, then pounded off into the jungle.

He sat motionless, listening to the bizarre woman crash off through the brush and doing his damnedest not to jostle the healing wound. The thought of turning jaguar and leaving, now, before she came back, was tempting. The thought of the pain of transformation while the injury stretched and tore was not.

He took a deep, careful breath.

She was very, very strange. Prone to fits of—well, fits. Yet, very attractive. He smiled, pulling up the memory of her appearance as easily as he could bring to mind her scent. Small, probably only reaching his shoulder, and delightfully curvy. Most of that was hidden under baggy clothes at the moment, appropriate for smashing through foliage, but every so often he could see the line of hip and breast pressing against cloth. Short hair, barely more than chin-length, riotously curly and pale, the color of sunshine on the water. Blue eyes, the hue of a cool summer sky. Fair skin that sported a dusting of freckles across an upturned nose, edging toward pink despite the overhead canopy.

She didn't seem inclined to hurt him. He'd scared the men off the night before—a partial change told him their scent was nearly twelve hours old. He doubted they would be back. Even if people talked about the jaguar-man, any hunt would be for nothing, and the furor would die down shortly.

He took another careful breath, closing eyes that seemed to be light-sensitive, swallowing against a headache. The skin around the gunshot wound felt tight, hot. Infected. In this jungle, it wasn't a surprise. Things would be fine. She'd come back, and he'd suggest they take the Jeep and go home. Things would be just fine.

Meg pulled her curly hair back into a nubby ponytail, only to have tendrils escape almost immediately and spiral around her face. The water from the pool hadn't been much cooler than the surrounding air, and now that she was on the way back to camp it seemed to have made the humidity that much worse. Her shirt clung to her, camouflage cargo pants—bought used at the Army-Navy store back in L.A.—almost indecent. Boots laced halfway up her calves protected her against any nasties, but made her toes feel damp. There seemed to be no way to properly dry in this soup.

She paused before entering the clearing. It had occurred to her that the man might be gone, that he could have fled as soon as she'd left, and then how would she prove to herself she hadn't dreamed the whole thing?

Her guides missing might be a clue, she supposed. Rope near the fallen tree could be another.

Meg took a deep breath, flushed when her breasts pressed against her damp shirt, and exhaled. Great. She took a bath to cool off and just ended up horny all over again. Damn it!

Steeling herself, she marched forward. The tent had collapsed in one corner. The ashes of the dead fire feathered out from the center of the clearing, surrounded by logs. The ground was mud, stirred up from many men living there for days, though most of the evidence of them—the packs, the tents, the food—was gone.

Just one man was still there, sitting against a tree. He opened his dark eyes when she walked up, black orbs surrounded by black lashes. He smiled. "I think," he said slowly in Spanish, "it may be infected."

"It? What? Oh, let me see." She leaned close to inspect the wound, bending over his shoulder. The heat of his breath whispered against her neck. Her skin prickled, nerves tingling up and down her spine. She ignored it as much as possible, peering at the injury.

It was pink, now, and inflamed.

"All right," she said firmly, settling back on her heels. "The nearest village is several days' drive. Think you can make that?" She stared hard at him, watched his gaze rise from the neckline of her shirt slowly up her throat, as solid as a caress. "Stop that," Meg said, but it lacked power.

He smiled slowly. "No doctors. My camp." His gaze still burned, and it wasn't the infection.

"I said stop that," she insisted.

His smile was slow, heady. "I can't help it," he nearly purred. "You smell nice."

Her skin beat in time to her heart, faster than it should have, warming with every moment he looked at her. "You're a—" she didn't know the word for flirt, "—charmer," she accused. Cats weren't supposed to flirt!

He laughed, a deep rumble that set her bones to humming. "Thank you." He looked pleased. "Now, about my camp?"

"Right," she muttered, dragging her mind back to the task at hand. An uncertain glance around the clearing revealed shadows pooling in the corners. "Thing is, it's almost dark. Think you'll live if we wait until morning?"

He smiled, as lazy as every housecat she'd ever seen. "I think I'll live."

She had never been great at cooking. Give her a rifle, she could hit a blob of spit at five hundred yards, but cooking? Well. There were other womanly pursuits. Like treasure hunting. Cooking was just one of the reasons she hired guides, after all.

She peered at the fire and the frying pan, certain there should be some brilliant way of hanging the frying pan so the contents—a can of beans—would heat. Nothing brilliant became apparent.

Then she felt warmth tingle up along her skin, awareness like that of a storm brewing. Turning her head, she was unsurprised to see that the deity had moved closer. He lounged alongside the fire, blanket wrapped haphazardly around his waist.

"Hi." Meg kicked herself for being dumb.

He smiled, slow and warm. "Hi. Can I try?"

It took her a moment to back off the lecherous "try whatever you like, gorgeous" response and think about what he was actually asking. Then her gaze turned to the beans. "Oh. Right." Happily, she handed him the pan.

It took some finagling as he worked around his injured shoulder, but a moment later he'd braced the pan in the smoldering coals, the handle wedged between two rocks. "Now," he said, gesturing with one graceful arm, "you can just stir."

"*I* can just stir?" Her Spanish accent vanished with indignation. "Why don't you stir?" Then she realized his face had gone white with pain, and she flushed. "Oh. Right. Well, that makes sense." Picking up a metal spoon, she gave the beans a single turn around. "Should you even be up and around? With that wound?" She eyed him critically.

He stared into the flames, pupils reflecting the light and glowing gold. "Probably not." An expression flitted across his face so quickly that Meg didn't quite catch it. His bare feet flexed, toes spreading and relaxing again. He looked at her sidelong, eyes turning black as the firelight left them. Liquid flame still slid over ebony hair, licking across strands like trapped gold. "Better than starving."

The expression had been mischief, she realized, and just resisted giving him a teasing hit. "Very funny."

His eyebrows lifted and dropped, a smile lurking playfully around the edges of his full mouth. "I excel at funny. Also..." he paused, eyes twinkling further, "...charming."

"I didn't mean you were *charming*," she pronounced, though she could feel amusement brewing. "I meant you were—" She couldn't think of a Spanish term. "Never mind."

He chuckled, the sound drawing Meg's gaze around as if pulled. His laugh was warm, unfettered, absorbed into the jungle as easily as the bird calls. He looked at her, still grinning, face transformed from wild beauty to comfortable lover.

No! Not lover! Freaky cat-man!

She wilted. Who was she kidding? He didn't look like a cat. Sure, occasionally he lounged like a cat, but mostly he was just too sexy for her good. "Tarzan might know the way to the ruins," she mumbled to herself in English, staring back into the fire.

"Hm?"

"Nothing," she answered quickly. "I'm Meg."

"Santiago." It rolled off his tongue the way Quetzalcoatl rolled off the natives' tongues, beautiful and exotic. She was vaguely relieved his name wasn't Tarzan.

"Nice," she said under her breath, then repeated the compliment in Spanish, still staring at the fire.

The jungle got dark rapidly when the sun fell below the mountain range. No leftover light edged down to them—it wasn't strong enough to defeat the layers upon layers of greenery. Animals went to bed while others woke, sound levels altering and changing, but never disappearing.

She heard movement, skin sliding over ground, and felt fingers brush her chin. Meg's breath caught. Her flesh warmed, the touch careful and delicate. He tugged, pulling her face around, and for a moment she had this crazy idea that she might tell him to back off, buddy, she wasn't that kind of girl.

Then she remembered smooth flesh over hard planes of muscle, and realized she really was that kind of girl.

She turned to face him, firelight sweeping across the angles of his face. Gazing deeply into her eyes, Santiago said, "If you stare at the fire you'll go night blind." Then he let her chin go and looked away.

Meg blinked. Waited, expecting a seduction at any moment. None was forthcoming.

That bastard.

She glared at him.

After a moment, he glanced over. "What?" He sounded confused and slightly annoyed.

She thought about reading him the riot act for not seducing her, but realized at the last minute that she might sound a little idiotic. Okay, a lot idiotic. "Nothing," she groused, and glared out at the blackened jungle. She could feel his eyes on her. She ignored him.

ꕥ

Breaking down the camp didn't take much. Unlike camping in the northern hemisphere, there weren't heavy tents or bear-proofing gear that needed to be dismantled. Nothing to keep them warm, not a whole lot of clothing to pack. Meg tossed things haphazardly into the Jeep, thankful that her guides had left it. When everything was as stored as it was going to get—she had no idea how to lash it all down, but it looked to her like it'd stay put—she went back for Santiago.

"Ready?" she called, wondering if he'd need help up or—

He rolled silently to his feet, holding the blanket around his hips with his good hand. Apparently, he didn't need help.

He moved with the same sleek grace that the predator he'd been two nights before had possessed. Once he passed, she turned to follow him, trying not to notice the way his broad back slimmed down to his hips, or the dimples along his spine that peeked just above the blanket.

"Can you turn back into a jaguar?" She didn't even try to be as quiet as he was while they tromped through the brush. "Like a rhino in Africa" sprang to mind.

Black hair fell over golden skin as he turned his head, looking back at her. Scars pulled across hard muscle, thin lines and larger, deeper marks. "Why?" There was a note of almost hidden suspicion in his voice.

She shrugged to convey nonchalance. "Just curious." Maybe he could only change at night. Except he'd changed during the day, when he'd been drugged. Had he been able to change as a child? And if so, could his parents change? He had social skills, so she very much doubted that, like Tarzan, he'd grown up in the jungle.

He edged gingerly onto the passenger seat of the Jeep, the lines around his mouth tightening as his shoulder moved. Meg hopped into the driver's side, starting the engine with a cough and a jerk. She winced. "Sorry about that."

Santiago said nothing.

Her mind turned back to the puzzle of the cat-man. If he hadn't grown up in the jungle, then he'd been in a village. Surely someone would have noticed him changing into a jaguar and reported it. Or maybe they knew, and had kept him secret. She glanced sidelong at Santiago, then turned her eyes back to the rutted path. And, of course, there was the science of it.

That didn't interest her nearly as much as the social aspect. After ten seconds, she got bored and dismissed it from her mind. His family was a fascinating concept, and she opened her mouth to ask. A look at his face silenced her.

His skin had gone ashen, his grip on the door handle tight enough to turn his knuckles white. His mouth was a thin, pressed line, and pain rode heavily in his gaze.

Meg faced front and worked harder to avoid potholes.

Chapter Three

"How far is your camp?" Meg rubbed the back of her skull against the headrest, itching at the sweat trickling across her scalp. Santiago's eyes were closed, but she knew he wasn't resting. His muscles were tense, beads of sweat standing out against his chest, along his temples, making his black hair damp. She dragged her eyes back to the road, scolding herself half-heartedly that this really wasn't the time to ogle him.

But lordy, he had a nice chest. Simply not looking didn't mean she couldn't remember it; all angles and planes, hard muscles and very little hair—just enough to emphasize shadows on golden skin. She thought of his purr, and nearly purred herself. She sighed. The weight of a gaze pulled her eyes back around, and she saw Santiago peering at her sidelong, a smile playing around the corners of his mouth as if he knew *exactly* what thoughts ran through her mind.

Clearing her throat, she shifted in her seat, suddenly warm. Okay, she'd been warm before, but now she was downright toasty. "Um. Your camp?"

"It'll be a while." His voice was like rough velvet stroking down her flesh. "A few days."

"Oh." Well, that was unexpected. Damn. "Maybe we should have lunch," she suggested, and snuck another look at him. He'd grown quieter as the day crept on, lines of pain slowly etching into strong features.

“Yes,” he rumbled. “That might be good.”

The nice thing about the jungle, despite bugs the size of small airplanes and heat like a volcano, was that you didn’t have to look for parking when you decided you were ready to stop. Meg stopped, stomped on the emergency brake, and declared them parked.

“Do you need help?” She glanced over at the man beside her.

Lips pursed, eyes staring straight ahead, he nodded once.

Concern threaded through her. In her experience, men didn’t admit to needing any kind of help. He must have been hurting.

“Hang on.” Unpeeling herself from the vinyl, she slid out of the car. He hadn’t moved by the time she got around to the other side, and she spent a moment wondering if he expected her to lift him out. Things could get awkward in that case. She supposed she’d at least cushion his landing...

Squashed under a hunka hunka burnin’ love. There were worse ways to go.

Then he twisted carefully, a warm hand settling on her shoulder for balance as he climbed from the Jeep. She didn’t move, trying to be as rock-steady as he might need. When his feet landed on the ground and he was no longer swaying, she came eye-to-pectoral with an utterly perfect torso. Sweat inched down the crease between his muscles, sped over the ridge above his abs, and slid helter-skelter down the center of a six-pack. Maybe even a twelve pack. It hit a snag in his belly button, worked its way out, and dropped past a flat abdomen before soaking into the blanket, which sagged low on his hips.

Meg swallowed.

Nope, she still felt utterly incapable of thought.

She licked her lips.

It didn't help.

She even cleared her throat.

She could still taste what she imagined he'd be like. Oh, God. She could *smell* him, all male and musk and something a little wild.

"Ready?" he asked.

She closed her eyes to break the spell. That worked. A little, anyway. Taking a deep breath she opened her eyes, staring straight ahead at his bare chest, her gut clenching in expectation. Her last boyfriend had hated it when she'd stared like that. Then she looked up—way, way up—into Santiago's face.

Full lips curved, black eyes warm, the sharp planes of his face softened by amusement.

Meg grinned and relaxed. "How's it feel to be a sex god?" she asked before she realized what was in her head. She blanched, then heard her words and knew *someone* was looking out for her. She'd spoken in English.

He lifted a single black eyebrow questioningly.

"Never mind," she said in Spanish, feeling a blush creep up her neck. "Lunch?" This time, she managed to stop any more sexual remarks before they left her mouth.

He could smell her, sweat and jungle and that indefinable female smell. Even worse, the very definable smell of lust. His shoulder hurt, and he somehow doubted he could do anything *about* the lust-smell, and yet it hovered in the damp air between them like some sort of drug.

On the other hand, at least he knew she was attracted, too.

Santiago sat, uninjured shoulder braced against a tree trunk, and watched her move from the Jeep to the spot they'd chosen. Her clothes brushed against her like a lover's hands, hiding and revealing with every step. He shifted his legs and tried to think about something less sexual. Trees. Trees were completely and totally nonsexual.

He'd had sex in a tree, once.

He cursed under his breath and finally moved, rubbing his injury against bark. *That* got his mind off the woman.

"You okay?" she asked in Spanish, frowning as she dropped a duffel bag of food on the jungle floor. "You look pale. Let me see your bandage."

"It's fine." His words were quick; he was half afraid that if she touched him it'd be more than he could stand. He knew she'd have soft skin, the hands of someone who spent most of their time indoors. Gentle fingers would glide over his shoulder and back, stroking down his spine as if he wouldn't notice—

Damn it. She hadn't even touched him and he'd lost the battle. Santiago shifted his legs, and the blanket with them, into a slightly more concealing pose.

"Don't be dumb," Meg said, apparently unaware of his dilemma. "Let me see." She'd already kneeled behind him, wedging herself between the tree and his skin, one leg tucked up against his ribs. He imagined her flesh beneath her clothes, soft and pale, muscles defined but not bulging. Delicate hands swept his hair out of the way, then skimmed down his shoulder to the medical tape.

He winced as she peeled it off, focusing on the pain to bank his arousal.

"Well, the infection hasn't gotten any worse." Her breath ghosted over his ear. She moved, her thigh brushing against his hip. His stomach tightened, and he resisted the urge to turn and see just how close her mouth was to his.

"Good." His voice came out in husky tones. Seemed like it had been husky since he'd first woken to find her kneeling before him.

"I'm just going to change this." She stood and strode back to the Jeep. Tossing the old bandage inside, she fished out a new, clean one, and walked back.

Santiago took a deep breath to settle himself, to steel himself for the torture about to come. Oh, God, he didn't know if he could take much more of this. She knelt behind him again and the very air seemed to warm. Then she rubbed cool cream over the wound, making the pain subside. Next came the cloth itself, and the worst bit—the tape. Specifically, the way she smoothed the tape over his skin, the pads of her fingers over his damp flesh, the occasional graze of a nail.

Just lust, he reminded himself, and a tourist probably wouldn't appreciate being bedded by someone she'd seen turn from a jaguar into a man. Besides which, it'd hurt his shoulder like hell itself.

He clung to that thought, even when the scent of heightened arousal spiked at his back. Damn woman. Then he smiled slowly, entirely too self-satisfied. Maybe in a day or two, when the infection was better, maybe she wouldn't mind so much being bedded by a Tezcatlipoca. She was certainly interested.

He angled his head to watch her over his shoulder. Her pupils were large in clear blue eyes, dilated despite the sunshine.

Definitely attracted.

Meg snuck glances at Santiago throughout their brief meal, noting that he only picked at his food. Granted, the food wasn't gourmet, but she'd seen men chow down through worse.

If his camp was several days away...well, she thought the infection was under control. But she kept thinking it wasn't bad, and then she'd actually *look* at it and be surprised. It had to hurt like hell. She guessed he had a ridiculous pain tolerance.

"Is there a doctor at your camp?" She hoped he'd say there was.

After a moment's pause he answered, "There's a curador."

She didn't know the last word, so she eyed him, waiting.

"Like a doctor," Santiago clarified.

Great. Some kind of crack-pot healer who'd feed him chocolate beans and declare him well. Not that she was skeptical. Of course, she was looking at a man who could turn into a jaguar. Or a jaguar who could turn into a man. Now *there* was a strange thought. Then she shook her head clear of confusion, and decided being a little less skeptical was probably wise.

Santiago stretched his neck, wincing briefly. Reaching up with his left hand, he rubbed the muscles above the gunshot wound.

"Hurt?" She flinched with sympathy pain.

He peered at her, a bare smile twisting his lips. "A little."

"Hey, I know sarcasm when I hear it." Smiling, she lifted her hands. "Is there anything I can do?"

He began to shake his head, hair spilling over his shoulders, then paused. "Distract me."

Meg valiantly bit back the sexual reply.

"Tell me about your home," he continued, apparently unaware of the thoughts his first words had caused.

Really, wasn't making lecherous comments supposed to be

a male thing? She pushed that from her mind and thought about home, settling back against a fallen log. Feeling a tickle, she turned and saw a trail of ant-like things, and leaned forward. "I'm from America. I mean, the United States." She hesitated. "Do you know about the U.S.?"

The look he gave her spoke volumes, all of it rounding back to the fact that he wasn't stupid.

"Right." She laughed. "And which one of us changes into a jaguar?"

The look dissolved. Amusement danced in his eyes. "*Touché.*"

A cat-man who spoke French. Huh.

"Wellll," Meg said after a moment, drawing the word out as she wracked her brain for something distracting. "My life isn't actually interesting," she finally apologized. "I'm a sociology professor at a university in Los Angeles—California," she added, uncertain that he'd know L.A. even if he did know the U.S. Then she mentally laughed at herself. Hell, L.A. had Hollywood; people who didn't really know where the U.S. was probably knew about L.A.

"Do you enjoy it?" he asked into her pause.

She smiled, nodding. "It pays decently, it's interesting, and it gives me lots of time off to come here."

He smiled briefly. "You come here often?"

"As often as possible," she confirmed. She grinned, growing animated. "There are possibly hundreds of ruins, just hidden in the jungle. After all, it's not hard to find stone markers where fields used to be cultivated. But the trees are so thick that you can't see far—you could walk within twenty feet of an ancient ruin and never know!"

Santiago listened, looking amused. "That could be

frustrating."

Meg sighed happily, just the thought of finding the remains of a civilization enough to make her heart go pitter-patter. She gave herself another moment of enjoying the thought, then pulled her mind back to the present. What else might distract him?

"My parents live nearby—I mean, close to me. In L.A. But my sister moved to Italy. Something about the food being better." She grinned and shrugged. It had been an excuse, of course. Maggie had really just wanted to move to Italy. "And..." She floundered, running out of things to tell him. "I think that's everything."

"I see. No boyfriend?"

She refused to let her smile dim. "I broke up with my fiancé almost a year ago. No one since him." Saying she'd broken up with him sounded much better than him breaking up with her, even if that was the truth.

Santiago's eyes softened, his head tilting. She had the distinct impression he saw more than a human could. "I'm sorry."

She shrugged, trying to not care. "It happens." If it hadn't happened more than once, for the same basic reasons—that she was, in a nutshell, too crazy—it wouldn't hurt so much.

"It happening," he said quietly, "doesn't make it any easier."

For a long moment Meg just looked at him, his golden skin mottled by shade, eyes nearly black. "Yeah." Her smile was without humor. "But you keep going, right? How about you? Do you have family?" She ran the sentences together, not wanting to talk about painful relationships, hoping she could distract him.

"Tragically," he drawled, "a large one."

She laughed, old pain falling away. "You don't mean that."

His eyebrows rose, a quiet snort huffing through his nose. "You obviously don't have a large family."

Meg relaxed against the tree again, feeling content, happy with life. "How many siblings?"

"None. But enough cousins to make up for it." Santiago's dark eyes sparkled.

"Pshaw," she scoffed. "I have lots of cousins. They don't count."

"Do they live with you?" he asked archly.

"No," she admitted.

"They count." He smiled, his expression warm. She felt herself respond, not simply lecherously—which was so easy with a half-naked cat-god—but something warmer uncurling in her stomach. Something she hadn't realized was missing until it appeared.

He shifted his weight restlessly, a long-fingered hand reaching up to rub at the cap of muscle on his shoulder.

"You all right?" She kicked herself for a stupid question. "Never mind," she muttered, eyes closed. "Just never mind."

Something tickled the back of her neck, and she shook her head as she sat forward. "We should probably get going. Your home is—" Something else tickled under her shirt. She squirmed, saw an ant-thing on her arm, remembered the trail on the tree, and screeched. "Oh, Christ!" she yelled in English, leaping up and dusting at her clothes. A bug fell from her curly hair onto her nose. Her voice hit ranges operatic sopranos would envy. "Oh, fucking hell!" Yanking at her shirt, she wriggled furiously to get it over her head before something started biting her or—worse—*crawling* on her. "Ew ew ew ew ew," she chanted into dirty material. She jumped at another tickle, cursing as she heard deep, masculine laughter, twisting vainly in an attempt to get the bugs off while still tangled in cloth.

"Let me help," Santiago said, still laughing, and she felt hands grab her shirt and yank it off over her head.

"So sick, so—so—gross—" she panted, still twisting and brushing, skin crawling with many-legged critters.

"Okay, hold still." Big hands skimmed over her flesh, rubbing away real and imaginary bugs. He moved behind her, brushing off her back, down her hips, over her rear, her legs, then up again to fluff her hair, chuckling the whole time.

"It isn't funny, you asshole," she grumbled in English, scratching at her arms, pale skin now exposed. She could have been embarrassed, but, hell, her bra was as decent as any bikini.

Santiago was *still* laughing, breath hitching across her ear. Then his fingers moved, tickling over her waist, sending Meg into a screeching burst of movement.

"You ass!" She leaped away and whipped around to glare at him.

His dark eyes were wet with tears, the hard planes of his face broken by a grin, muscles rippling above the blanket he'd tied around his hips. He clutched at his stomach with both arms, wheezing, "Ow, ow," through every few hilarious breaths.

She stared at him, arms crossed, ignoring the fact that she was wearing her granny bra and khakis slung low on her hips. "You're a dickhead," she said in English, wishing she knew how to say it in Spanish. The locals had refused to tell her.

"I'm sorry." He shook his head and tried in vain to control his breathing. "I couldn't resist."

"Try." But her ire fled and a traitorous smile lurked at the corners of her lips.

"I will. I'm sorry." Santiago grinned unrepentantly, bending to pick up her shirt with his good arm. He shook it out, checked it for bugs, and handed it back with a sweet sort of look. "Forgiven?"

Meg glared at him, grabbed her shirt out of his hand, and checked it over herself. "This time," she growled, but couldn't keep from laughing when she looked up.

His dark eyes twinkled, mouth sliding into a warm smile. He reached out, brushing a curl out of her face and tucking the lock behind the shell of her ear. "Thank goodness." His voice was nearly a purr once more. As natural as anything, he leaned in and kissed her. His hand eased around the back of her head, threading through her hair, cupping her skull.

She pressed into it, his full lips gentle over hers, soft and still smiling, tasting like sunshine.

He broke it off first, pulling away only a few inches before smoothing his thumb over her jaw.

"We should, uh, go." She winced. "I mean. We're supposed to be getting to your village, right?" Oh, man, her parents would be proud of her. Restraint! She could manage it on occasion.

"Right," Santiago agreed. He stepped back, hand drifting away from her skin, fingers trailing the edge of her jaw.

Right. Damn her restraint! She nodded firmly and headed toward the Jeep, refusing to acknowledge that her legs wobbled. That was just foolish, anyway.

ᘓ

"Why ruins?"

Meg glanced away from the road when Santiago spoke, pushing her sunglasses up on her head. It was really bright without them. She dropped them back down onto her nose. "I don't know. Why not?" She could feel his gaze on her even when she turned back to navigating the rutted path.

"'Why not' isn't a reason," he said after a bit. "With that logic, you could just as easily have taken up bull fighting."

She grinned. "Maybe I'm a world-class bull fighter." She expected a snort at best, an annoyed eyeroll at worst.

He laughed, effortless and clear. "I feel honored, then. What's your bull fighting name?"

She maneuvered the Jeep carefully around a hole, chuckling. Oh, he would be easy to fall for. "You caught me. I'm not a bull fighter." She looked at him, more to see his warm black eyes than anything, and answered his original question. "I remember being thirteen and seeing a special on Egyptian ruins. They fascinated me—the way people might have lived, what scientists could tell from the simplest of things, how much remained a mystery." Meg smiled, remembering that breath-held feeling, watching with excitement and awe as each new piece of the puzzle went together. "I think that got me into sociology, but I never had the patience for the grunt work you need for the research." She liked the find, the excitement, wondering what might be around the next tree or down that stretch of river.

"Why didn't you go to Egypt?" Santiago asked softly.

She glanced at him, surprised to realize he seemed honestly interested. Something inside her loosened, relaxed. She leaned back in her seat, flexing her fingers against the steering wheel. "Too expensive."

"So it's just the dollar that brings you here." His tone was dry.

A bright blue and red bird soared through the trees, and Meg smiled, watching it. "No. Things are still wild, here. Where else can you go that's so alive?"

"The Congo?"

She laughed. "Sure, the Congo. But it's even more dangerous than coming here, and costs more."

He reached out, fingering a curl of plain blonde hair—the bane of her existence—before he spoke. "It can be dangerous here, too."

One shoulder lifted in a negligent shrug. "I'm careful. And I can take care of myself." The rifle was a constant presence, heavy in the back of her mind.

"Ah, yes. I forgot about your bull fighting abilities."

White teeth flashed as she grinned. "Hey, don't knock it. If I can take down a bull, you in your jaguar skin?" she teased. "Not a chance. Much less a human."

Santiago laughed, tipping his head back and roaring. Birds screeched in the canopy, monkeys calling from a distance away. Meg couldn't help but respond, lips curling upward. When his hilarity finally died down, she glanced over at him. "So, what do you do?" She half expected him to say he worked in the fields, or something of the sort. Seemed like most of the people here did, and yet it would have been a disappointment.

"I own a business," he said with a smile, left hand reaching up to rub his neck above the gunshot wound.

"Oh?" She remembered the little shops meant for tourists in the city, and the smaller, more run down stores that served the everyday populace. "What sort of business?"

He rolled his head on the headrest, turning to look at her. "We make boats."

She brightened. She supposed it really shouldn't matter

what he did, and chastised herself accordingly. Still, it was nice that he wasn't a schlep. "How cute!"

At his silence, she looked over. He seemed amused, heavy eyebrows quirked. "That's not a term normally applied to me." The corner of his mouth twisted upward.

Sheepishly, she shrugged. "Sorry, it's just..." She really couldn't dig her way out of this one; changing the subject seemed the better part of valor. "How long have you been building boats?"

He hesitated, head tipped, gazing off into the middle distance. "Maybe fifteen years," he said at last.

Meg thought about that for a while. Too short to be a family business; not passed down from his parents, so... "Do your employees know about your—" She wiggled her fingertips, then pointed at him. "You know."

"Fingers?" he asked blandly.

"No! Your cat thing."

"Only my family knows," he said quietly. "And you." It didn't sound like an honor when he put it like that.

"I won't tell," she said, almost frustrated.

"Thank you."

No one would believe her, anyway.

ꙮ

At Santiago's request, they stopped early for the night. The constant jostling was making his shoulder ache. He padded from the Jeep to the small clearing his traveling partner was setting up in, grabbing at his blanket just before it slipped off his hips. Pausing under a large tree, he watched dappled sunlight glitter off Meg's pale hair and skin. She hummed, crouching in the damp ground to light a fire. Santiago smiled, the pain of his shoulder forgotten for the moment, his attention caught as she tucked back a curly lock of hair only to have it slip forward again. She was bedraggled and dirty, but perfectly unselfconscious in her grime. He liked her all that much more for it; too many women he knew fussed and primped and were horrified at the thought of a little dirt.

Not Meg.

She glanced back over her shoulder, overbalancing and dropping to the ground. "Are you okay? You need help?"

He stepped farther past the tree, shaking his head, feeling his hair slide over his shoulders. "Just thinking."

Her face lit when she smiled. "About what?"

He couldn't tell her that he'd been thinking about *her.* "That song you were humming. What was it?"

Her smile faltered. "I was humming?"

Santiago chuckled, settling down on the ground beside the fire. Smoke kept the bugs away. "Yes—something a little cheerful. It was..." He paused, then mimicked it, his voice wobbling.

Her good mood spread across her face again, and he smelled her arousal spike the tiniest bit. "Oh—it's a commercial jingle."

He didn't know what he'd expected, but it wasn't that. Santiago laughed. She was gazing fondly at him when he stopped, and he gave her a quizzical look.

"Nothing. You just—" She blushed and shook her head, smiling.

"What?" Now he was curious. "I just what?"

She stood, heading back to the Jeep that was almost

hidden by the foliage. "You just have a nice laugh," she called over her shoulder.

A grin spread across his face as he watched her vanish into the shadows before appearing on the other side of the trees.

It was dangerous to like a human. Human women found out what he was, and they got scared. Granted, Meg already knew what he was, and she didn't seem scared, but...

She'd responded really well to that kiss. It was easy to remember, the heat of her skin, the softness of lips. He was a fool.

She was humming when she returned.

"Is that also a commercial jingle?" Santiago asked, amused.

She chuckled. "Afraid so. I think those might be the only tunes I know."

He grinned, comfortable in her presence in a way he hadn't been with others. It helped, Santiago thought, that she knew what he was. He didn't have to hide. It would be frowned upon by his family, by the rest of their little village, that he'd been found out...but he realized he didn't mind that so much. It was good to be himself. "I'll have to teach you some new songs." He let his voice deepen into a near purr.

Her pupils dilated. He could smell the warmth of her skin. "I bet you know all sorts of songs I've never heard," she said mischievously.

Santiago smiled a promise. "I bet I do."

All they needed was wine to make the evening completely goofy. Meg cracked up as Santiago launched into another verse of a song she was *certain* wasn't real. No one sang about phallus-shaped oysters. "Stop!" she cried, her sides hurting from too much laughter. "Oh, please just stop!"

He did, dark eyes twinkling with mirth. "You said you wanted to learn something new."

She laughed harder, shaking her head. "I didn't know you were going to sing *that*!"

"I'm offended," he said with mock disdain. "That happens to be a masterpiece in Santa Diega, I'll have you know."

She couldn't remember the last time she'd had so much fun, or been so comfortable around someone this attractive. Sure, he was a cat-god wearing nothing but a blanket, but somehow it seemed perfectly natural. The fire crackled merrily at her back, the pan they'd eaten out of sitting to one side, silver gleaming liquid gold with the light. "It's a pity I can't translate all my dirty songs," she said, grinning at him. "I'll have you know I'd make you blush."

Dark eyebrows lifted. "Oh? I doubt that."

She chortled, certain of herself. "I would. You'd be *horrified*." And the fact that she was even contemplating trying to translate them said something—she tried not to be obscene with new men, really. Tried even harder to let them think she was sweet for at *least* a week.

Okay, five days.

Well, really, if she aimed for three she usually made it.

Oh, all *right,* two.

He leaned in conspiratorially. "I know a song about dolphin sex."

"I know one about three men and a pig," Meg shot back.

He peered at her from the corner of his eye. "All right. You win."

She laughed, delighted when he grinned. "I lied," she admitted after a minute, completely unrepentant. "I don't really know any songs about barn animals."

Santiago sighed, a hand over his bare chest as he looked skyward. "Ah, teasing me and then admitting it's untrue. You break my heart."

"It's a woman thing." She nodded cheerfully. "We promise dirty songs and then yank them away when you get hopeful."

He chuckled, the sound rumbling through the forest. "Yes, because every woman I've met can outdo me in bawdy songs."

When she glanced over, his smile was warm and dry. She wasn't sure if she should be embarrassed and stop now, or just go with it. She decided to go with it. "You're obviously not hanging around with the right women!"

Santiago's dark eyes were warm, black in the starlit night. "Obviously," he agreed, his voice nearly purring with amusement.

Heat curled through Meg at his steady gaze. He didn't blink often, and when he did it was slow, thoughtful. Cat-like.

Insects hummed, rubbing together wings and legs to make music. Night birds fluttered and called for each other, while small mammals rustled through the trees. The fire crackled, spreading light and warmth, soothing and lending the night a sense of safety.

Or maybe that was Santiago and his easy laughter, bronze skin golden in the whispering firelight. It could have been him soothing Meg, setting her nerves at ease, tugging free humor and warmth with gentle smiles and graceful movements. Him providing the sense of safety, an unspoken promise not to turn away because she was too wild.

There wasn't anything wilder than him.

"I can't remember the last time I had so much fun with a man," she said in English, mostly to herself.

Santiago tipped his head, watching her out of feline eyes,

full lips turned up in a careless smile. He answered in kind, in a language she didn't know, something a little sharp and alien.

"Is that your native tongue?" she asked in Spanish, looking at him.

He nodded once.

"What did you say?"

"What did *you* say?" An eyebrow quirked up.

She hesitated, then felt her skin go warm. "I said I was having fun."

He smiled slowly, then placed one foot flat on the jungle floor, toes spread. Balancing his weight over it he leaned in, brushing his knuckles across her jaw.

The night was quiet, waiting. His hand slid around the back of her neck, toying with a curl there. Meg could feel his body heat, just as warm as the fire, the whisper of his touch sweeping over her skin. Then he closed the last of the distance, lips brushing hers delicately, then harder, increasing the pressure. She shivered when his tongue grazed her lower lip. Opening her mouth, she tasted jungle and their dinner, and something a little wild that could only be Santiago. She put her hands on his waist, felt the tremor that went through him when their flesh touched. The kiss deepened, demanding softly, teeth nipping at her mouth before pulling her bottom lip into moist heat. She groaned, moving closer, skimming her hands up his body, over smooth skin sheathing graceful muscle.

Mouth and teeth teased the line of her jaw, tipping her head back until he could nuzzle under her ear, breath shivering over the shell.

She wasn't supposed to have a fling with a crazy cat-god, Meg told herself weakly. Really.

His fingers skimmed over her collarbone, barely touching,

arousing in their gentle caress.

"Oh, this is bad," she sighed in English. This would be the death of her. His touches would undo her, and then where would she be? "Hell." She'd deal with the consequences later, because this was—

Santiago jerked back, pulling away as if burned. The smile he'd worn earlier was gone, replaced by hurt and then, quickly, anger. His expression closed down, dark eyes going cool as he sat back. "We should sleep." His voice was flat. "We have a long drive tomorrow."

Meg blinked, bewildered. The night air, sultry before they'd started, seemed cool without his body heat. Or maybe that was just the chilliness she was getting from Santiago. Hot one moment, and ice the next.

She watched him, confused. *Men.*

Chapter Four

They might have made better time walking, Santiago thought as the jungle edged past at glacier speeds. If he could have changed and gone through the trees, he could have made much, much better time. Of course, the transformation would nearly incapacitate him, and his foreleg wasn't working so well in his jaguar skin. As a human, the gunshot wound shifted far enough that it wasn't crippling. Perhaps more importantly, as a human he didn't need to walk on his hands.

The silence stretched between them. His mood darkened. He shouldn't have kissed her. Shouldn't have started anything, should certainly not have been lured by warm conversation and those addictive smiles she gave so freely. Shouldn't have been fooled by her easy laughter, or the way she looked at him out of smoky blue eyes, like he was both incredibly sexy and just plain good to be around. So, he'd had a more enjoyable night than he could remember in a long time; it didn't mean anything.

Not when she knew what he was. Knew his shapes altered at whim. She was polite and considerate, he growled at himself, but polite and considerate didn't mean *interested*, not even when he could smell her damned arousal.

Humans disgusted him. Their stupid brains short-circuited things that should otherwise be easy. She liked him, he liked her, that *should* be the end of it. But no, no her mind had to remember that he wasn't human, that he'd turned from a cat into a man, and doubtless her mind insisted she should avoid him. It was what they all did, when they found out what he was. Fear him, avoid him, tease and then withdraw when it became serious.

He glared at the passing jungle, wincing when they hit a rut. He felt a snarl deep in his chest and buried it. Pain burned in his shoulder and down his arm, making his mood even fouler. He hated women. He hated human women. He hated the fact that none of his own people, not one of the Tezcatlipoca were the least bit attractive to him, and that instead he found himself falling for this woman who reacted just the same way the others did when things got serious.

Maybe she'd get used to the idea with time.

And he hated himself for hoping that. Humans and Tezcatlipoca didn't mix well. He had learned that the hard way. Repeatedly.

"Santiago?" Meg said, fingers tapping on the wheel. "You okay?"

"Fine," he bit off, pain making his voice tight.

"We could stop, if you're hurting—"

"I'm fine." The sooner they got to his home, the sooner she could flee. He should never have kissed her.

Just the thought of her cupid's bow lips made his groin tighten, heart picking up speed. Cream colored skin, smooth and without scars. Freckles like bits of gold dancing over her nose and cheeks.

Fuck, he had it bad. Realizing his teeth had shifted to fangs and his lips were pulling up off them, he took a deep breath and forced himself to relax. He should never, ever have kissed her.

Meg kept half an eye on Santiago, part of her annoyed with the snit he'd fallen into the night before and still hadn't come out of. The other part of her was worried. She knew his shoulder hurt, could tell by the tiny shifts of weight, the tautness of his muscles. She really wanted not to care, since he was being rude. First he kissed her, then he snubbed her—Christ. Maybe cat-gods thought they were above manners, but *really*.

She tapped her fingers against the vinyl steering wheel again, turning it to edge around a pothole, eyes scanning to find the smoothest path through the rutted road. It'd serve him right if she hit every hole she could find, she groused. She didn't, though, only too aware of the pain it would cause. Pain wasn't ever funny. The thought of it might be satisfying, but the reality…

She sighed. Too bad.

They killed time with the quiet between them. Meg hummed, wishing for a CD player. She glanced at Santiago, and glared at him for a moment before turning away. He didn't notice.

She'd given up her ruin hunting for this? A moody cat-god who couldn't even be civil? She added "sulker" to the long list of things she *didn't* want in a lover, and drove on.

༄

"We should probably stop for the night." It was the first thing he had said since that morning. Or, more accurately, since their kiss the night before. Wait, no, Meg realized snidely. He'd said other things. He'd said, to be specific, "fine". He'd said that a lot.

She glanced at him, her own temper simmering. "Sure." She kept her tone neutral and yanked the wheel to the left. Her earlier musings on pain never being funny had given way to frustration and resentment, and the angry part of her relished the way the car jerked.

Santiago winced. Then his full lips thinned to a white line, and he pulled himself from the Jeep.

They set up a small camp and made dinner in silence filled by jungle calls. Shadows deepened as they ate, encroaching on the little light cast by their fire.

She stared into the flames, glaring harder when she felt his eyes on her and remembered his caution about night blindness the first evening. Screw him and his night blindness warnings.

The movement of skin against cloth prompted her imagination, and suddenly she could see him, still brooding. The mental image added fuel to her fire, and she spoke before thinking. "You're a grown man." She shot a glare toward where he sat. "Stop sulking!"

"Sulking?" Santiago's voice cracked in the darkness. "I'm not *sulking.*"

"Oh, don't give me that crap. You've been sulking since we kissed. And I know I'm not a bad kisser, so it isn't that I didn't live up to expectations."

"No," he said, rich voice a sarcastic purr. "You lived up to every expectation I've learned, thank you."

That stopped her. She thought back, trying to figure out if she should know what he was referencing. She finally decided that, no, he was still just being an ass. "If you're going to make snide comments, you should at least make sure I know what the hell you're talking about." And to think she'd been falling for him the night before!

Again, she heard the sound of movement, the blanket

rustling. Then a shape formed out of the gloom, tanned skin picking up licks of firelight. His eyes were black in the shadows. "Women," he said with disgust. "You're all the same. It doesn't matter what you say or imply or do, you don't really mean it."

She was flabbergasted.

He continued, "You could at least refrain from kissing *back*, if you find me that appalling."

He wasn't making any sense. She looked at him like he'd grown fangs. Which, granted, wasn't impossible, but he hadn't. "You have lost your ever lovin' mind," she said in English, then added in Spanish, "What are you *talking* about?"

"You! This—this disgustingly *human* tendency to idolize anything abnormal, and then fear it when it proves to be true!"

"Now I fear you?" she asked skeptically. "You're kidding, right? I fear you, so I kissed you?"

"I disturb you, so you overreacted when *I* kissed *you*. A simple refusal would have more than sufficed." The sneer in his voice didn't quite cover the hurt.

Confusion doused her anger. She blinked into the dark, able to make out parts of his face as the firelight danced over him. "What are you talking about?"

"'Hell,'" he quoted through gritted teeth. "I wasn't going to bite you."

Meg stopped the "too bad" remark before it left her mouth. "Of course not," she said instead, still baffled.

The fire crackled in the following silence.

"Wait—" she began, stopped, and considered her words. "You thought I didn't want to kiss you?"

Anger fell away, beaten back by uncertainty. "Well... Yes."

She watched him, eyes becoming accustomed to the dark. Wariness chased hope chased caution across his strong features. "You're this gorgeous Latin man," she pointed out slowly. "*Why* wouldn't I want to kiss you?"

"Because I'm a gorgeous Latin *cat*-man?" he suggested. "And..." he paused, then bulled forward as if mentally ticking off points, "...you're not interested in bestiality? You don't think it would be a good idea? You're worried you might be allergic? It's simply too much for you to handle? I might maul you? The thought is repul—"

Meg shook her head once, and he fell silent. "Are you *serious*?"

He didn't answer, one hand holding his blanket around his waist, the other tense at his side.

"God. You are serious," she muttered. When she spoke again, she enunciated. "I didn't say 'hell' because I was disturbed. I said it because I'd been *trying* to be a good little girl and *not* jump you, and you were making it really damn hard."

His features twisted through a parade of expressions. Relief won. "Oh."

She smiled, rolling her eyes. "You're an idiot. Sit down."

He did so, settling in next to her.

Leaning back on her hands, she considered his profile. "Women don't tend to like the whole cat thing, huh?"

He slanted her a wry look. "Not exactly. It...ends relationships."

Meg winced, seeing the carefully hidden pain. "Well, I think I'm over it," she drawled. "Now, maybe if you had turned into a jaguar and tried to kiss me, that would have freaked me out. But as long as you're human... Hey." She grinned and lifted a single shoulder in a half shrug.

"You are..." He hesitated, then chuckled. It chuffed through the air between them, warm and a little surprised. "Unusual."

"I could have told you *that.* In fact, I've been hearing it most of my life. And you," she bit off, "do you always jump to the worst conclusions?"

She could feel his gaze, even if she couldn't see it. "Can I make it up to you?" he asked, voice low and warm.

She shivered at the near purr, and fought the temptation to tease. She was just as tempted to climb into his lap. "Well, it depends." Her eyes twinkled. "How did you plan on doing that?" It was easy to remember the laughter of the previous night, the camaraderie that had come so naturally.

"I could start by apologizing," he suggested with a warm smile.

She gave that a great deal of mock-consideration. "Well, it's a start," she said dubiously.

A dark eyebrow arced upward. "What else would you suggest?"

Oh, she had all *sorts* of suggestions. She tried to keep them PG rated. "You could teach me that oyster song." Okay, PG-13 rated.

Santiago laughed, and the last of the tension fell away from between them, absorbed into the jungle. "Is there anything else you'd take? That song is a trade secret, you know."

Meg feigned a heartbroken sigh. "Well, I suppose I'd consider another kiss," she said before she'd even thought about it. That kiss had started to be awfully nice...

Santiago's smile was slow and sweet, just a little bit dangerous. "You're sure it doesn't bother you?"

"What doesn't bother me?" she asked, then realized he was talking about the cat-thing again. "Hell no," she said emphatically. "I think I'll manage." She inched closer, lifting a hand to run the backs of her fingers down his forearm. The thought that someone had hurt him—possibly several someones—made her heart pound with anger. Funny, she thought absently, watching firelight flicker over his skin. She'd never wanted to protect someone before. Especially not someone as physically able to protect themselves as Santiago.

Light spilled over his flesh as he moved, creating patterns and shadows where there were none. He edged closer until she could feel his body heat pressing up against her.

"I don't even know you," he said, sounding a little frustrated.

Meg snorted and closed the rest of the distance. "Don't you know guys aren't supposed to *want* to know someone? Guys are just supposed to have mindless sex all the time."

He laughed, dark and quiet. "Of course. I apologize. Whatever was I thinking?"

"And you're still talking." She ran her hand up the back of his neck, pulling him down toward her for a kiss. His lips were warm, soft without being feminine, his hair silky under her fingers. Then his arm rose, hand splaying across the small of her back, spreading heat and making rivulets of pleasure cascade down her spine. He moved her effortlessly, single arm tightening and pulling her closer until her hip pressed in against his. All thoughts of warm softness evaporated in that single tug, his carefully restrained power suddenly obvious in the ease with which he brought her near.

She squeaked at the initial pull, unused to someone strong enough to do as they pleased. Her hands tightened, one on his neck, the other on his good shoulder. A chuckle rumbled through his chest, and snuggled close against him she could feel as well as hear it. Heat spread throughout her body like lightning, skin electrified. Santiago's nose skimmed against the sensitive skin under her earlobe. Meg's breath broke. She tipped her head, giving him better access. His fingers brushed up and down over ribs and back, spreading easy, warm pleasure. She lifted her own hands, stroking along muscled arms, testing her nails over elastic flesh stretched taut across planes of muscle.

"You know," she said, then stopped to kiss golden skin, nipping at his neck before tonguing the mark. He tasted like salt and musk and something she could only describe as masculine warmth. "I've never liked long hair on men before."

"You're suggesting I cut it?" Santiago asked, amusement in his voice.

"God, no." She ran her hands across his collarbones, down the front of his chest, feeling him shiver when she caressed a perfectly muscled torso. "It makes you look a little wild."

"You like wild," he rumbled, the words not quite a question. She looked up and saw teeth, white and gold in the firelight, as he grinned.

"I love wild," she admitted on a sigh. It had gotten her in more than a little trouble at times.

His voice dropped to a purr, the words felt as much as heard. "I'm good at wild."

A shiver fled through her body. "I just bet." Wherever he touched her felt hot, fire sizzling along her skin. And he seemed to touch her *everywhere*.

Then he stopped touching.

Meg wriggled. She nudged. Then she twisted around to peer up at him.

"Shh." His eyes glowed with reflected firelight. He sat predator-still, focused on the jungle, and if he'd had pointed ears she would have expected them to be perked.

She checked his ears. They weren't pointed.

Animals and bugs went on with life around them, undisturbed. She remained quiet for as long as she could. An eternity. Two eternities, even. It was probably at *least* ninety seconds. "What?" she whispered.

Santiago's stillness broke, and he looked down at her with vague annoyance. "Which part of 'shh' didn't translate?"

"Asshole," Meg muttered in English. But he'd already stopped paying attention to her, focused once more on the wild surrounding them.

Then he moved, finally, rising to his feet and tangling their fingers. "Come," he said, still staring elsewhere. "This way. Quietly."

Even though she wanted to, Meg didn't point out that she wasn't exactly equipped to move quietly through a jungle. He'd figure it out soon enough.

He didn't get the chance to figure it out. A man stumbled into their clearing, gun leveled, shouting in Spanish too rapidly for her to make out words. All she could see was the barrel of a rifle, gleaming in the firelight, slick with oil and weaving through the air. He shouted again, his face flushed.

He couldn't have been more than twenty.

"Santiago," Meg said quietly, then again, louder, "Santiago!" She didn't know what she was going to tell him, or if she was going to tell him anything. His grip on her hand tightened and he began to tug her in another direction, then pulled her to a stop before she'd even taken a step.

Her head whipped around, a question on her lips. She froze.

Another man stood in the shadows of night and trees, waiting for them to move. When he spoke, it was slowly.

"We'll be taking your car," he said simply. "Your food,

your—" He paused, smirking at Santiago's near-nudity. "Your clothing, and any valuables."

This wasn't the eighteenth century, Meg thought, and there weren't highway bandits anymore! Besides, highway bandits only happened in Europe, and this wasn't even a highway! Santiago did fit the romanticized idea of a large, manly man, she supposed. If he did the romantic, old-world thing and tried to leap on the gunmen she was going to kill him herself.

"Take them," Santiago said.

She stared at him. He wasn't even going to argue?

In her peripheral vision, she saw two more men appear from the jungle, surrounding the small clearing. She edged closer to the bulk of the half-naked man beside her, as if he might be able to stop bullets. They really should have camped farther from the road.

"And her," the ringleader added.

Meg turned to stare at him. "Fuck you," she said in English. Santiago's grip on her hand tightened.

"No." The cat-man spoke flatly.

Everything slowed. Or she sped up, she wasn't certain. The ringleader raised his gun and Santiago twisted toward her. She had a moment to think, *He looks heavy*, before his body slammed into hers, carrying her to the ground. Shots rang out, explosively loud, cracking through the forest. Then Santiago was moving, off her, arm bones twisting, tendons writhing under his skin. Fur spread from his hand—no, paw, claws extended like serrated talons—up to his elbow. Only it wasn't quite an elbow anymore, and he wasn't quite a man. Not a cat, either. Something in between. Something terrifying and wrong, in an instinctive, visceral way that the sight of a twenty-year-old with a gun could never induce.

He roared, angry, the king of the jungle letting loose an

inhuman call. People shouted, the bitter scent of fear mingling with the rot of the foliage. A gun fired, and then something caught in Meg's shirt, lifting her up—up above the forest floor, up into the trees. Cloth tore, the seams catching under her arms and holding, her feet scrabbling for purchase. Muscles on the beast flexed and shifted, neither human nor cat, and his grip changed, holding her more securely before they flew out along a branch that bent and moved under their combined weight.

She finally screamed.

The cat leapt, caught the next branch with claws digging through moss, into bark, tail whipping madly for balance. Then they were lunging forward again, taking paths no human could, at speeds no animal should.

The sound of gunfire receded, replaced by the drum hammer of her heartbeat ricocheting in her skull. She clung to skin or fur depending on the moment, biting back a cry when they fell, only to climb again a moment later. They sped through the jungle, panic lending power, and then the beast leapt onto a mammoth wall. He caught, two feet and one hand, the other claws tangled in her shirt. They hung for a long moment, a hundred feet above the ground, bark slowly shredding.

They were going to plummet. She knew it as surely as she knew her own reflection or that annoying mole on the bottom of her foot. He couldn't climb holding onto her, and the only way was straight up or straight down. Meg twisted to stuff the toe of her boot into a knothole, giving herself just enough of a boost to loop her arm around Santiago's shoulders. "Go!" she yelled, wrapping both legs around his waist.

His arm swung up. Hand shifted to paw, body twisting, sinew popping and rippling beneath her until a jaguar scaled the side of a tree. Claws splayed, his muscles bunched and shoved, gaining inches, tendons in his paws and forelegs straining.

Power coiled in his hips and back, releasing and springing them higher. They landed in a nest made by boughs branching outward from the trunk, the tree so large that there was more than enough space for them.

He changed before they hit, suddenly as human as he'd been cat, now soaked with sweat.

Meg landed hard, scrambling to get her feet under her. A spreading branch stopped her dash, solid under her shaking hands. Her breathing smashed through her lungs. She couldn't seem to calm down. Couldn't quite breathe fast enough. Adrenaline made the nighttime colors sharper, clearer. The faint breeze against her face felt deliriously cool.

"Are you all right?" he rasped, breathless and concerned.

She glanced at him, dark hair plastered to his neck, black eyes scrutinizing her. "Those men—they were—" She couldn't say, "Going to kill us." Instead, she said, "You're—you just—" She couldn't say, "Changed to a jaguar and dragged me through the forest." Instead, she said, "Naked."

He glanced down as if to check for himself. When he looked back up, he was smiling. "You notice the damndest things."

Panic receded. She smiled shakily, shrugged. "It's a talent." Then everything hit, and she realized she was going to be ill. He must have realized it too; he grabbed her, hauling her over his lap and hanging her off the side of the nest. Meg retched, fingers digging into moss and bark. Even her toes felt drained. When she was done Santiago pulled her back across his lap, holding her tightly.

"They were—they—" she began, but still couldn't complete the thought, couldn't complete the sentence.

"I know," Santiago whispered, strong arms drawing around

her, fingers in her hair. "I know. We're safe. It's all right."

Meg had never been a hysterical sort. Of course, she'd never been threatened at gunpoint, either. Or dragged through the trees by a cat-man. She figured she was overdue.

How long she sat there, curled against a warm chest, shaking and just trying to breathe, she didn't know. It was still night when she finally calmed, though. Santiago stroked her hair, his heartbeat slow and heavy under her ear. She spread her hand over the pectoral she wasn't leaning on, feeling the skin thump with blood. Healthy and alive. She flexed her fingers, watching flesh give, muscles hard beneath.

Shock made her chilly, but when she shivered he just held her close, smoothing his cheek along her hair. The world came back quietly as she started to think again.

The animals called. It wasn't until she heard them that she realized they'd been missing. Moonlight filtered through the jungle canopy, diffuse and silver by the time it reached them. Something cried out, and something else cried back. Leaves whispered, blending with the sound of Santiago's breathing. His scent—cinnamon and musk—curled around her, changing the warm air, dancing along her skin. Rubbing her cheek against his chest, she felt his hand stroke down her curly hair, strong fingers massaging the base of her neck. His legs moved, reminding her of his nakedness and strength all at once. She sighed.

"You know," Santiago said, voice rumbling through her bones, "if you didn't smell like vomit right now, I'd kiss you."

Meg grinned, closing her eyes. "Well, if I didn't smell like vomit right now," she replied, the last of her tension draining away with their gentle teasing, "I'd let you."

Chapter Five

While sleeping curled up against someone was comforting, it wasn't actually conducive to getting much rest. Meg awoke just before the sun rose, though she didn't move from Santiago. If she stretched, she could reach the tree trunk. She peeled bark off and, trying not to think about bacteria and disease, chewed on it like a primitive toothbrush.

She wasn't particularly tall, but neither was she a waif. It had been a long time since she'd been able to curl on a guy without them complaining, eventually, of their legs going to sleep. Since he was still snoozing, she supposed his legs were okay.

The night before drifted through her mind, detached and a little unreal. In fact, watching Santiago go from cat to man seemed more real than being attacked by bandits with guns. The flight through the jungle was almost lost in a blur of fear and darkness, and she didn't try very hard to remember it.

Leaning against his chest, it was easy to forget. Easier when his hand rose, drifting over her spine and down again. She turned, glancing up at him. His eyes were still closed. Mostly asleep and *still* sexy. Damn him. Still, far be it from Meg to pass up an opportunity like this one.

She stroked his biceps, fingers grazing over bare skin. His hand slid up her arm and over her shoulder. She had to say this for the cat-god: He smelled damn good. Even unshowered. Turning her head, she inhaled his warm, masculine scent. It seemed completely natural to open her mouth and see if he tasted like he smelled. Her tongue brushed over the ridge of his collarbone, sweeping into the hollow between tendons and down, below his Adam's apple. Heat curled through her skin and pooled in her gut. God, he *did* taste as good as he looked.

His hands moved, one sliding down her hip, under her thigh, fingers wrapping around the back of her knee and repositioning her effortlessly. She nearly squeaked, reaching up and linking her fingers behind his neck as if he might drop her. The fact that he was sitting down apparently didn't matter to instinct. When she looked up at him again, his eyes were open, pools of darkness soft and sensual. His head dipped, brushing a sigh away from her mouth.

"Morning," he said, voice a vibration against her. He closed the distance between them before she could respond, teasing her lips open, stroking his tongue over her teeth.

She didn't usually groan, but right then she *might* have made a girly, mewling sound as his tongue slid wet and hot against hers. Hands stroked over her shirt, molding it to her skin, memorizing every curve and line. It felt electric, heat following everywhere he touched, warming her from the inside out. Meg lifted her legs and settled them again, something primal whispering a need to move, to wriggle closer.

Instead she threaded her fingers up into his hair, pulling him in, feeling silken strands fall over her hands. He purred, deep in his chest, and she felt an answer tug in her stomach. Santiago released her mouth, brushing his nose lightly across her face, barely a heated breath from her cheekbone. He followed the line of her cheek, down her neck, to the junction of throat and shoulder. She squirmed, turning far enough to press her breasts against his chest, rubbing slightly when pleasure spread from her nipples to her groin. Hands slid down her back and under her shirt, and she arched into him at the sensation of skin against skin.

She liked sex. She liked it a lot. It had never felt like this, though. Nails tested the resiliency of her flesh, strong fingers flexing briefly. The power contained made her shudder, her head dipping to nip at the cap of muscle on his shoulder.

He tensed, then picked her up and moved her until she straddled his lap. His extremely naked lap. She sat back, running her hands down the center line of his chest, watching his nipples tighten and his pupils dilate. She reached his stomach and pushed back a bit farther, letting her nails skim over abdominal muscles. They quivered under her touch and his fingers stroked up the outsides of her thighs, hot and distracting. He leaned in for a kiss and she smiled, leaning back out of reach. A satin black eyebrow rose, amusement in his eyes.

"I'm checking you out," she said with an impish grin.

His hands fell away from her thighs, linking behind his head, stretching his torso up sinuously. "Please, check away," he purred.

Meg ignored the way his voice made her shiver and completed her downward caress. Down past his abdomen, onto the smooth muscle of his pelvis and to infinitely more interesting regions. He was already hard, skin like satin over steel. She brushed her thumb over the tip, feeling utterly powerful when his whole body twitched, breath catching in response. She grazed her fingers over his erection, then more firmly, rubbing her thumb over the crease of thigh and hip.

His hands came back down, grazed up the backs of her legs to her rear and flexed. "You," he said raggedly, "are going to kill me."

"Only if you're very, very lucky." Then his hands tightened and he pulled her close again, fingers going around to the front of her waistband.

"I'm at a disadvantage here," he said against her mouth, nipping at her lower lip.

The button on her pants slid free, the zipper inching down with a purposefully slow *click click click*. Meg twisted to unlace and pull her boots off, then decided to forget seduction and wriggled out of her pants and underwear, too.

Santiago dragged her back down before she could yank off her shirt, his hands around her ribs tugging her close, holding her up so he could lick at her belly button beneath the hem of her shirt. She eeped, hands curling on his head, hoping he'd move down or lift her up or *something* that would put his mouth just a tad lower on her body—but instead he let her slide down him, nuzzling under cloth until she felt his erection hard against her. She shuddered as she dragged across the length of it, body tightening with anticipation.

Hands edged under her shirt, inching it carefully off over her head, teasing at stomach and ribs and then only barely touching breasts as he disrobed her. He lipped at the edge of her bra—and *why* did she have to be wearing a granny bra? Next time she came to South America, she was packing a thong and something lacy, damn it!

It didn't seem to bother Santiago in the least. He tossed her shirt over a branch and unhooked her bra, sliding it slowly down her arms, fingertips brushing her skin.

"Much better," he murmured, dragging his tongue over one dark nipple. She bit back the whimper, shifting her hips to rub against him. He sucked on the nub, sending shivering spasms into her stomach, pulling her breast into his mouth. One hand slid down her back, over her hip, dipping between her legs. He touched wet heat and rubbed slowly, callused fingers sliding across soft, slick skin. Every line in her body drew taut. Then his free hand skimmed up her ribs, cupping her other breast, circling the nipple with short nails. When his teeth closed oh-so-carefully on the one in his mouth, his fingers tightened, tugging, sending pleasure splintering through her like light through stained glass.

"Oh, God," Meg breathed, "do that again."

She felt more than heard him chuckle. A tongue pressed against her, warm and wet, sliding before rubbing against the hard peak of her nipple. Much lower, fingers skimmed over warm flesh before slowly entering her. Heat spread and she twisted, felt him push another finger in, brushing against the knot of nerves. She swallowed a cry, muscles trembling, surrounded in the scent the two of them made. Then his hand withdrew and his head came up, leaving her cool and bereft. She started to protest—right until his hands on her hips pulled her in and down, and she felt his erection push slowly into her body. Meg inhaled sharply, feeling herself stretch as he filled her. Santiago paused, leaning close for a kiss, and pulled her the rest of the way down.

She almost whimpered as he completed the movement, sheathed inside her so deeply she thought she'd never lose the feeling. Her pulse pounded in her throat, in her breasts, where their bodies joined. His hands ran up and down her back, soothing and arousing all at once, sliding down the crease of hip and leg to rub his thumb against wet flesh, making her groan and tighten around him.

"Okay?" he whispered against her sensitive lips, their breath mingling.

She managed a nod before he moved, a hand under her hips lifting her as he rose to his knees. Her fingers locked around his neck and she squeaked as he pressed her down onto bark and moss, driving deeply into her with the motion.

"Oh, good," he breathed just as she groaned, "Oh, God." Then he started thrusting, long, powerful strokes, filling her every time he slid inside and leaving her wanting more as he withdrew.

Meg wrapped her legs around his waist, changing the angle slightly, helping him to penetrate deeper. Muscles flexed under her hands, the body above her taut with power. She lifted her hips, matching him thrust for thrust, tightening as he pushed in, stretching her, hitting every nerve she had. Ecstasy shattered through her body as she rode a wave of sensation like she'd never felt before. It promised light and darkness and everything in between, and she crashed with it willingly, tumbling into wave after wave of pleasure with a heartfelt cry. She felt Santiago thrust one last time, one hand pulling her hips up into him, pressing against her and sending spears of sparkling white desire through the waves already buffeting her.

The orgasm seemed to last days. It left her drained, sleepy, energized and wired all at once. She lay for a long moment, letting the world come back, aware that he hadn't rolled off but also wasn't crushing her.

"That," she said on a moan, "was wonderful."

"Mm hm," Santiago sighed into her neck.

She started to shift, catching her lip when he slid out of her and caused another shiver to cascade down her spine. She moved sideways—and was stopped by his hand on her arm. "Don't do that," he said, black eyes solemn.

Blinking, she frowned and hoped he wasn't one of those men who turned into a Neanderthal after sex. At his pointed gaze, she looked sideways.

As the yawning abyss six inches to her right became

suddenly obvious, she understood why she shouldn't do that. She also screamed.

"We *are* in a tree," he pointed out, smiling wryly as he snaked his arm around her shoulders and pulled them both straight up. "Cat-like balance and reflexes notwithstanding."

"As long as there're no barbs." Meg took refuge in wit as she scurried away from the edge of the nest they'd slept in.

"Sorry?"

Pale skin flushed bright red. "Nothing." Afterglow neatly sideswiped by the fear of falling, the world—and reason—started to intrude.

She'd just had sex with a man in a tree. And while that was alarming enough, she'd done it without a condom, and without even *asking* about disease. Now she was going to go home and have an HIV baby. And her parents would never let her hear the end of it. Not, at least, until she died a slow horrible death of tuberculosis and AIDs. Of all the *stupid...*

She found her underwear and pants and, cringing at the thought that now they were going to be messy, damn it, she put them back on. Her bra came next, then she yanked her shirt over it. One boot sat nearby. The other had seemingly vanished. It wasn't like there were a lot of places for a boot to hide; it couldn't be under the bed because *there was no bed.* She tried not to curse herself for a fool again. "Where's my boot?" she bit out, not really expecting an answer.

"Below." There was an odd tone to Santiago's voice. Meg gave him a sharp look, but then ignored it.

Carefully, she leaned over the side of the tree and saw her boot nestled between two roots far, far below. "Fuck!" She scraped hair out of her face.

"It's all right," he said, and that odd tone was still there. "We have to go down anyway."

She was still berating herself as twelve kinds of a fool—even if it *was* far and away the best sex she'd ever had—when she turned to look at him and stopped at the blood streaking his arm. "Oh, God." She winced. "We need to re-bandage that." She couldn't remember it bleeding so much before. Maybe *right* after he'd been shot, but not recently.

A black eyebrow rose. "With what?"

"The Jeep—" Then she realized, and wilted. "Is probably long gone. Right. Well..."

"Home isn't too far," Santiago said. "We'll be fine."

Meg nodded once, and turned away to look down at her boot. It was easier than looking at him. God, she already wanted him again. But she'd proven herself an idiot; even she knew better than to have unprotected sex, no matter how attractive the man. She wouldn't repeat that mistake.

Given that he was completely naked—his blanket gone with the gunmen—and that he had to change into a jaguar to get them out of the tree anyway, Santiago figured it would be easier if he remained in cat form. Amazingly, him turning into a cat didn't seem to bother Meg past the initial curious inspection. Since she seemed to be in a snit—he had no idea why, and, since his injury had torn, was in entirely too much pain to find out—he figured conversation wouldn't be good, anyway.

He didn't quite know what had gone wrong. She'd seemed to enjoy herself plenty during the sex. Maybe it had been too fast. He admitted he'd gone quicker than he did with most women—something about her had driven him right over the edge—but she'd seemed perfectly eager, and it wasn't like she hadn't orgasmed. In fact, he could very easily remember her legs wrapping around him, pulling him harder into tight, warm—

He snarled at a branch just to snarl, annoyed with the physical reaction he couldn't control. You'd think tearing open a bullet wound through changing, flight, and sex would be enough to put a damper on his libido. Apparently not.

So, it wasn't the sex she was annoyed about. Maybe it had been the tree. Maybe she had a tree hang-up. "You may have sex with cat-men, but never in trees." Hell, he didn't know.

Pain blazed down his foreleg, and he could feel heat starting to boil under the skin. Infection. Sleep and sex had helped him to ignore it, but now it rose to the surface and demanded he pay attention.

He decided he wasn't too manly to limp, if it made the injury hurt less. He knew *some* healing had taken place, or he wouldn't be able to walk on it at all, but he'd be damned if it felt that way. He was whining and stopped, pausing to glance back and see how Meg was doing. Or if she'd heard him. He hoped not. Whining cats almost always induced syrupy-sweet cooing.

She'd been following him as he broke a trail through the jungle. Leaving a visible path went against every jaguar instinct he had, but it would take them days to get home otherwise. She was still silent, brooding, reeking of frustration. Or maybe it wasn't the scent that tipped him off, but the way she stomped through foliage. Hard to say, really.

Santiago turned and kept going.

Hunger interrupted her brooding, but the food, she thought dourly, was with the Jeep. While her stomach gnawing up its own lining took her mind off stupidity—and, just as important, how hard a time her parents were going to give her if there *were* repercussions—it added to her overall bad mood. The fact that she grew warm every time she thought about that morning didn't help matters any. God, *why* did he have to be so good at sex? Why couldn't he have been a dud in bed? Or in a tree, as the case may be. But no, he was gorgeous, sweet, interesting, and sexual dynamite. Of all the luck!

The day was edging toward afternoon when she realized the jaguar—it was a little odd to think of him as Santiago—stopped just ahead and sat down, injured foreleg held slightly off the ground. Blood had soaked through his fur and dried, leaving rust-red to mask the black rosettes.

Meg stopped as well, itching at a rash of bug bites along one arm. She had no idea if the demi-god understood Spanish in cat-form, and felt a little silly talking to him regardless. Then, between one eye blink and the next, he wasn't a cat.

She took him in with a single long look, heart picking up speed at gold skin stretched over a muscular frame—

Except it wasn't all gold skin. In fact, his face looked almost gray and his shoulder was crimson. "That doesn't look good," she said.

He glanced at his wound, grimaced, and looked elsewhere. "I'll live." But Meg noticed he didn't get up, just stared at nothing for several minutes. Then he cleared his throat. "I thought we should take a break."

Since he didn't say it was for her, she didn't point out that he seemed to need it. She just settled on a fallen log, brushing away plants and bugs, and waited.

He was gorgeous. She was angry all over again.

He tensed, annoyance and irritation as clear as if he'd screamed it. "Would you mind telling me what I did?"

She glanced at him, at his shoulder, and snorted. "Got shot."

"I mean," he said through gritted teeth, "to make you angry."

She opened her mouth to say "nothing", realized it was a lie, and cursed softly in English. It wasn't—entirely—his fault they'd had unprotected sex. "No condoms, and I'm not on the pill," she snapped with frustration.

Animal noises marked the silence. When she finally turned to look at him, he was staring at her incredulously out of black eyes.

"That's *it*?" he asked, barking a laugh.

Anger boiled. "Oh, sure, easy for you to say! You're not the one more likely to get diseased or end up with a kid!"

Still laughing, he shook his head and held up a hand for truce. With difficulty she settled, eyes still narrowed to slits. He had about thirty seconds to either treat this with the appropriate concern or explain why he wasn't—to her satisfaction.

"I'm not *human*," he said at last, grinning. "First off, I'm clean, and second, if I weren't—we can't give each other diseases without some mutating germs and probably a blood exchange. As for *children*—while it's not impossible I could get you pregnant, it would take a whole lot of trying."

She rolled her eyes. "And virgins can't get knocked up the first time."

He slid off the log, rolling up to his knees to look her in the eyes. "If I got you pregnant, then we'll decide what to do and do it. But it's not likely. Cross breeding is almost unheard of."

Most of the heat spilled out of her gaze, but she glared at him anyway. That knowledge did make her feel better. She wasn't sure she believed him entirely, given that—as far as she knew—he didn't have a medical degree with an emphasis in cat-god and human procreation, but it helped.

If he'd grown up with people like himself, they'd *probably* know. "Are the other people in your camp like you?"

He nodded, moving back to sit on the forest floor, one leg propped up. It left nothing to the imagination. She admired the view. "They're all Tezcatlipoca. We all change." He hesitated, then added, "Except for my grandmother, who says it's hard on her old bones and refuses to go human again." He smiled and shrugged with his good shoulder.

But the smile was strained, and despite the intense awareness Meg was feeling at his nakedness—she kept remembering the touch of his hands on her skin—he seemed completely unaffected by being watched. Well, stared at, really. And he was pale. And sweatier than he should have been, even given the heat.

She leaned forward and put the back of her hand to his neck, just under his jaw. "You're hot."

His half smile faded. "Infection," he said quietly. "We should be at my village soon."

Nodding, she stood. "Tell me if I can help."

Santiago stood as well, cradling his injured arm against his chest. "Not unless you can manage a sling."

Her heart leapt into her throat as she reached out a steadying hand to help Santiago through another stumble. She hadn't realized how graceful he was until, over the course of the evening, that grace had eroded. It frightened her more than she cared to admit. If his motor control was being affected, he was worse off than he wanted her to think. Infection spread fast in the heat and damp.

"Come on," she said, edging beneath his uninjured arm and supporting his weight until the jungle demanded they separate.

"We're almost there." She had no idea where they were, or how far they had to go, and kept praying that one of the last things he had said—he knew where to go, and his people would catch their scent if they got even remotely close—was right.

Despite her ignorance, she kept spouting the reassurances. The lie spilled from her lips, offering encouragement, hope, and a gentle prod.

A branch scratched across her bare upper arms, her shirt having turned into a sling when the infection had gotten worse and the pain had increased past the point of his ability to manage it. She doubted very much the sling helped other than as a mental balm, but if it kept him going...

He staggered again, nearly sending them both to the forest floor. "Santiago!" she yelped, stumbling hard under his weight. "Come on, 'Tiago, you've got to get up." Not that he was down—not entirely—but she was pinned between a tree and a very large man.

"'Tiago?" a voice echoed curiously.

Meg jumped, bashing her head against moss-covered bark and staring furiously into the darkness. Images of more armed men superimposed themselves in her mind's eye, sending her heart racing.

Then Santiago spoke. It wasn't Spanish. Something she didn't recognize, something with a great many consonants. Then she heard her name mixed in, and a shape stepped out of the shadows.

"You speak Spanish?" a man asked, bending to take Santiago off her.

Meg started to caution him that Santiago was heavy—taller than this new person, and with more muscle—but in the next moment she realized it didn't matter. Lifting him didn't seem to bother the stranger.

"I—uh—yes," she said finally. "Please tell me you're from his camp."

He blinked at her out of black eyes. Family trait, she supposed, and yet somehow his eyes didn't seem quite as fathomless as Santiago's. Black, sure, but more like coffee and less like a promise.

He nodded once, then turned and started off through the forest. That was when she realized he was naked.

Well, hell. Santiago was naked except for a sling, and Meg only wore pants and a bra. It wasn't like any of them were particularly modest.

She hurried to catch up.

Chapter Six

The stranger moved faster than a normal human, but he didn't turn into a jaguar and run off so Meg didn't complain. She stumbled over and around bracken and brush, doing her best to follow the stranger's non-existent trail. He carried Santiago easily, tossed over broad shoulders like a sack of flour. Santiago wasn't objecting and that, more than anything, alarmed her.

The stranger didn't speak. She didn't have the breath to try. All her energy went toward fighting past trees and brush. One branch in particular seemed to have it out for her, and she struggled with it furiously until it at last gave way, spilling her into a tiny meadow. She staggered to a halt when she saw a fire.

People poured out of the jungle, melting free of shadows. Most of them were naked. A few had lengths of cloth wrapped around them, tied above shoulders or around waists. The material was filmy and gauzy, always looking half ready to fall off though none of it did.

Voices babbled in a language she didn't recognize, something that wasn't Spanish, wasn't English—wasn't even Latin-based, as far as she could tell. Small fires dotted the ground, people rising from seats near them.

Someone—no, some *jaguar*—landed softly ten feet away, muscles rippling as it stalked forward. Strength gathered as it prepared to pounce, sinew bunching under a sleek coat. Meg squeaked, and a moment later the stranger who had carried Santiago was between her and the cat, and then the jaguar was a man, and the man was glaring at her. The stranger spat out several words, and both men looked at Santiago.

Meg looked, too.

They'd stretched him out beside the logs surrounding the small blaze. A teenager held his head in her lap, carefully dribbling liquid from a wooden mug down his throat. An old man with gnarled flesh and twisted bones crouched next to him, muttering to himself. Grizzled gray hair was tied back at the nape of his neck, his bare skin painted with tattoos, while beads and claws hung around wrists, ankles, and neck—protective amulets or some such, she supposed. As she watched he took a flask made from what looked like a giant nut and poured water over Santiago's injured shoulder.

Santiago shouted and pushed upward, but the old man practically sat on him, chattering away angrily.

Meg's memories of scolding grandparents merged with scenes from The National Geographic Channel, and she had to stifle the urge to giggle. She suspected it might sound a little hysterical, anyway.

It seemed everyone had arrived. There were maybe fifty people, including two women—one barely more than a girl—with babies. Still more people waited above, at ease in the branches over the jungle. It was then that she noticed the—well, the term houses certainly didn't apply. Constructions meant for sleeping, she supposed, banged together between boughs. In some cases they were only held together with rough rope, and they all looked terribly impermanent. Despite appearances, moss draped across the closest ones she could see, proof that they'd lasted long enough for the jungle to grow up around them. Paths wound from branch to bridge to tree, claw marks on all the trunks. Here and there jaguars stretched in the shadows, eyes glowing yellow with reflected light. She shivered and looked away.

None of that was as important as the man beside the fire. With a final glance upward, she tore her eyes away from the darkness and started toward Santiago, who mumbled in the language she didn't know.

Someone stepped into her path, and she recognized the man who'd stalked her in cat-form a moment before. He snapped words at her, canines too long, his eyes holding a threat.

Meg stared at him. Funny, she was pretty sure he'd said something dangerous or rude—maybe both—but it didn't have much impact when she didn't understand. "I have no idea what you just said to me," she replied in Spanish, "but I'm going to make sure Santiago's all right." They were probably pouring tepid water on him, adding bacteria to infection. She didn't know what she was going to do if that cynical thought was true.

She strode past the short, stocky man, feeling his gaze burning into her back, knowing she'd just become the focal point for the entire village.

Village, she realized faintly, not a camp like she'd thought.

The old man looked up as she neared the fire, then looked back down at his charge and kept lecturing, his bony knees pressing into the strong chest below him.

Santiago was flushed, his sweat-drenched hair sticking to his forehead, eyes glazed. Still, he managed to grumble something that earned him a nose pinched between the swollen joints of the old man's index and middle finger. Meg suspected "All right, all right, I'm sorry, I'm sorry!" translated pretty well in this case. The old man let go. Then he looked up, rheumy eyes narrowing, and spat out a long string of consonants.

Meg threw her hands up. “I don’t understand you!” she said in frustration. He said the same string of consonants, very loudly and very slowly. She sighed.

“How long has he been sick?” a soft, female voice asked in Spanish.

Meg jumped and looked around. The barely-a-woman waited, holding a fussing baby. “Oh,” she said. “Uh, a few days. He was shot.”

The woman translated, and the old man nodded before dribbling more liquid on the wound. Meg started to protest, then froze. Alcohol fumes wafted up.

Santiago cursed. A lot. At least, Meg was pretty sure that was what it was. The old man’s gray eyebrows rose, and the teenager holding Santiago’s head giggled and turned pink.

Meg crouched, resisting the urge to reach out and touch the prone man who, just twenty-four hours before, had been healthy and strong. “Will he be all right?”

“Hector thinks so,” the girl-woman said, crouching as well. “The people don’t like you being here, though,” she added, dark eyes catching and holding Meg’s gaze. “Who are you?”

Meg stopped a wince. How was she going to explain tourist?

༄

A child stared at her across the rough wooden floor, watching her eat. His big black eyes were framed by thick lashes, his pudgy cheeks pressed firmly by the hands bracing his head up. “Do you know Britney Spears?” he asked in halting Spanish.

A wooden spoon stopped halfway to Meg's mouth. They'd understood L.A. a lot better than she'd expected. "I think she might be on a different coast," she pointed out gently.

The six-year-old rolled his eyes. "You don't know *anything*," he complained, and slid off the chair to skulk away.

She paused, re-examining what she *did* know, and finally had to admit very little of it involved Britney Spears. She ate another spoonful of soup, or at least the soup-like substance, before Frieda came in.

Frieda, who had cheerfully confirmed her name wasn't remotely Spanish, was just as young as she looked. Despite her age, she had two children, was one of the best Spanish speakers in the group, and the person most comfortable with Meg. A long discussion the night before had sent Meg's assumptions about their culture out the window; the people in this village were not only in touch with the outside world, but happily used what modern conveniences they could, and even traveled abroad.

"How's Santiago?" Meg asked, food forgotten.

Frieda smiled, dark eyes creasing, and dropped several dead rabbits. Meg scooted quickly out of the way. "Fever's broken," Frieda said. "Hector thinks he'll be just fine. Santiago did more damage to the wound than he needed, what with changing, but it'll heal now."

Meg relaxed, finding a smile, her stomach flopping. "Thank God," she sighed in English. Not that she *really* cared. Hell, she barely knew the guy and he was some strange not-human/cat-thing, so really it didn't matter—

She stopped. She couldn't even lie to *herself* convincingly. But whether or not she cared, it didn't matter. He had family, a life here, and—

She chewed on her lower lip. She wouldn't mind living here.

Okay, she decided, eyeballing the dead rabbits, she might mind some of it after a while. She was no Jane to his Tarzan.

She shook her head at herself. She was completely jumping the gun. Overreacting. Aside from a few nice moments and pretty good sex—okay, really great sex—he hadn't said he liked her. So...

So, nothing. Her circling mind just kept running around those same thoughts over and over again, worrying at them but not giving her anything else.

"Are you all right?" Frieda asked, hair falling to one side as she tipped her head to catch Meg's gaze.

Meg smiled, but it felt small and painful. "Fine. I think I'll just get some air."

"All right." Frieda offered a reassuring look.

Meg wondered what she needed to be reassured about. Then she was outside of the little cabin-like tree house, swinging around and down on branches carefully grown into a ladder shape.

The jungle heat was oppressive, settling down over her shoulders and pressing on her back. The thin length of cloth from Frieda was wrapped around Meg's torso, tied over one shoulder. Even as light as the material was, it stuck to her damp skin, catching on her upper thigh every time she took a step.

She ignored the stares from the Tezcatlipoca as she hopped off the branch-ladder and made her way across the small clearing, boots clomping on the ground. The cat-people might think nothing about walking barefoot around here, but she didn't want ooze squishing between her toes. Gross.

Children laughed, tossing a ball made from twisted branches around, dashing between trees. A jaguar lying in the bit of sun in the middle of the clearing snuffled and stretched, claws extending before they retracted again. One sleepy eye opened to watch Meg pass, then closed again, showing gray hairs speckling the lid.

Hector lived in one of the few homes on the forest floor, rather than in a tree. They'd taken Santiago there, laying him out on the rough wood that kept the damp from coming in. There was no door, just an opening where people came and went. Meg hesitated, then brushed aside the flap of skin that served as a screen, peering into the darkness. The old man was nowhere in sight—only Santiago, stretched end to end across the single room.

He lay on a mat, sleeping, his breathing slow and even. Thick eyelashes brushed like shadows against his cheekbones, bronze skin glowing in the stillness of the hut. Sweat pooled in dips and hollows of muscle and bone, and two fingers twitched as he dreamed. Long black hair had been washed and brushed at some point in the night, and now it lay glossy and smooth underneath strong shoulders. His lips parted, and he snorted.

Warmth unfurled in Meg's stomach. The scene wasn't at all romantic, yet she found herself smiling, relaxing against the doorway. It reminded her of his humanity, bringing back the nights they'd spent together, everything from the laughing conversation to the feeling of closeness to the fabulous sex. Not having to hide who she was, or pretend modesty she didn't feel, enjoying the way his quick mind worked—all of it combined into something that simply fit. It made her comfortable. He made her smile. The realization came upon her slowly, like sunshine cresting a hill and spilling softly into a valley below. She was in love.

Silly, since she'd barely known him a few days. She couldn't stop the smile from racing across her face, or the way her heart began to thump. She *was* in love. She had no idea what she was going to do about it, but it was there. Imagining living without the cat-god in her life was like imagining the world would end at sunrise: theoretically possible, but an idea she couldn't give substance. She was completely and totally head over heels.

Someone cleared their throat, and she jumped and stepped aside, still grinning like a loon.

Hector gave her a suspicious look and slid into the hut, keeping to the edge of the floor, his hands full of herbs. With one eye on her he tore the leaves and roots into small bits, dropped them in the bowl of rubbing alcohol, then put strips of cloth in to soak.

"I love him," she told Hector, even though she knew he wouldn't understand.

Bushy gray eyebrows drew down and he glared.

"I know," she said, as if Hector had responded. "I don't get it either. But I think I probably loved him the instant I saw him." She paused, thinking. "Well, maybe not the *very* instant, since he was a jaguar and that would be a little sick. But the instant I saw him as a man." She thought about that. "Okay, no, at that point I was too tired. But the first time I saw him as a man during the day." Yeah, that covered all the bases. She grinned again. "I love him."

Hector continued to glare at her.

Meg hugged herself—someone needed to—and realized that all was right with the world. In the face of a realization like she'd had, everything else seemed miniscule. Whistling, she turned and headed out.

She had ruins to hunt for.

They didn't like her. Even with the language barrier, it became obvious when they stopped speaking if she walked up.

She didn't really care. They'd have to come around, because she wasn't leaving. After the brilliant epiphany she'd had two days before, she wasn't letting Santiago go for anyone. Not anyone. Not unless he woke up—and she really wished Hector would stop giving him sedatives, no matter how much the healer insisted he would mend faster if he slept—and told her to go away. If the words came out of Santiago's mouth, she'd do it. But she didn't think that was going to happen.

She grinned, recognizing her expression as sappy even without the benefit of a mirror, and crashed through the forest. Every time her mind wandered she remembered something little. Something like the way he'd smiled at her that first day, still-yellow eyes seeming warm, full lips tipped up at the corners. The way his fingers felt against her chin when he'd pulled her gaze away from the fire. Talking into the evening, his voice a purr along her skin, soothing and beautiful. Laughter, unbridled and easy.

Why she hadn't realized this whole love thing earlier, she wasn't sure.

A mud puddle yanked her out of her musings. She pulled her foot out of the hole, shaking off the worst of the grime, grateful to have boots. Then she changed direction, stomping through the jungle again. She was getting quieter, she thought proudly. Now she only sounded like a dozen elephants, rather than a herd. She was also getting better at sneaking through the foliage without having to chop it all down.

She wondered what her parents would think of Santiago. They'd like him, of course. She was certain of that. Would he tell them about being able to change into a jaguar, or would that be a secret between them? Maybe—

She ran into a fleshy wall. Backpedaling quickly, she looked up. And then up farther.

God, she sure appreciated the whole "let's run around naked" thing going on in this village. Except this particular god-man didn't look happy. Neither did the one behind him.

Her skin prickled, hair lifting off the back of her neck. "Can I help you?" she asked in Spanish.

The one in front started to talk, and the one behind began to translate.

"It's time to go," the one behind said, smirking.

She forced her expression pleasant, if cool. "Thanks, but I can find my way back to the village."

The one in front listened while the translator did his job, then he shook his head and spoke again.

"Frieda said you have a plane to catch. It's our job to make sure you get there safely."

She glanced around, then forced her gaze back to the men. "That's all right. I'm just going to get a later flight."

"You already know Santiago will be fine," the translator said. "Time to leave." He stepped to one side, jerking his chin toward a spot behind him. "We brought you a car."

Through the trees, she could make out one of the snaking dirt roads that linked the villages, and the red of a Jeep. Her Jeep, she suspected, and she wasn't sure she wanted to know how they'd gotten it back.

"Thank you," she said calmly and firmly, "but I'm going to wait for Santiago."

The two men exchanged pitying looks. The one in front slouched to the side, leaning against a tree trunk.

"Santiago," the translator said, "already has a family."

"Yes, and you're all very nice—" she began, but the man

spoke right over her.

"A wife and children. Here. You should go before you upset them further."

The ground dropped out from under Meg. The man in front grabbed her biceps, steadying her. Had a family? Wife, kids? That wasn't possible. They'd—he'd—

Bile rose in her throat, and she swallowed it back. Insects buzzed, too loud in the overheated jungle. He had a family. Maybe they did things differently here. Maybe having a fling on the side wasn't unheard of. Maybe—

"Maybe I should go home," she murmured through numb lips.

The two men nodded. The grip around her arm tightened, supporting her as she staggered out of the forest.

"Who?" She didn't resist as they handed her up into the Jeep. Hot vinyl burned her thighs, and she put her hands under the sensitive skin for protection. The car started with a jerk, coughing to life and rolling down the dirt road.

"Frieda," the translator rumbled, sitting behind them in the bed of the car.

So the boy was his. And the baby was his. And of course Frieda. She was young and beautiful and kind. The road blurred, and Meg sharply blinked back tears. She lifted her chin, refusing to look back at the jungle and the village behind her. She wouldn't cry for him. She barely knew him, that much was painfully obvious. Barely knew him, and had only met him a few days ago. She wasn't in love. No one fell in love that fast.

She dug her fingernails into the undersides of her knees, and tried to ignore the tightness in her throat. She wasn't entirely successful.

Chapter Seven

"This is an interesting premise," Meg hedged, twiddling her pen between thumb and index finger, "but you might want to narrow it down a little."

Her student's face fell. "But narrow it down to *what*?" There was a whine in the girl's voice.

Meg grasped her rapidly failing patience with both metaphorical hands and hung on. "Do a little research on this topic, and I'm sure you'll find something." Unless she was an idiot, which Meg hadn't yet ruled out. But professors weren't supposed to say things like that out loud, so she bit the inside of her cheek and closed her door firmly when the girl left.

She collapsed back in her chair, staring at the bland cream-colored ceiling of the university office. She needed a painting up there to stare at. Something green. A jungle scene.

She grimaced and straightened, fixing her eyes on the pile of papers to be graded. The last thing she needed was anything that reminded her of the jungle. Christ, it had been two weeks since she'd come home, it was a week and a half into the semester, and she couldn't stop thinking about...all of it. But most especially, she couldn't stop thinking about Santiago.

She didn't want to think about him. It hurt too much.

She'd had blood work and a pregnancy test done, and everything was as he'd said: no diseases, no babies. Nothing to tie her to him except half a dozen days—not even that—out of the thousands she'd already lived. Surely the hurt would fade with time. It was what she told herself when her mother asked what was wrong or when her colleagues said she was acting oddly and maybe she should use her sick days.

It would fade with time.

Her vision blurred, and Meg closed her eyes. She wouldn't cry. She hadn't cried since she'd gotten home, and she sure as hell wouldn't start now. She *wouldn't* cry. And if she said it often enough, she might even believe it.

Taking a deep breath, she opened her eyes and stared at the papers, willing herself to read them. They were only a line or two each—ideas for the essay due at the end of the semester. It should have been easy enough to go through them quickly.

She stared at them for another five minutes, all focus lost as she remembered the way Santiago felt, the musky, male scent of him, the brightness of his black eyes.

Cursing herself, she stood and gathered her things, stuffing them into her briefcase before heading out the door and down the hall. She could do this at home, and if she needed to zone out for a while she could do that, too.

"Dr. Westfield," the department secretary called as Meg stormed past. "Meg!"

She glanced back over her shoulder, pausing with her hand on the doorknob. "Can it wait until tomorrow?"

Amy hesitated, then nodded. "Yeah. It's not an emergency."

Meg shoved her way outside.

ꟾ

That night Meg drank too much wine. Her students paid for it the next morning despite her best attempts to be civil. She locked herself in her office during her hour break, swallowing two Aspirin and hoping they'd kick in quickly.

Someone knocked.

She sat, silent, willing whoever it was to go away.

"Meg, a Mr. Valdez has been trying to contact you," Amy called through the door.

Meg frowned. "I don't know a Mr. Valdez," she snapped.

"I'll tell him," Amy answered, and footsteps retreated.

Meg groaned and let her head fall back against her chair. Now she owed Amy an apology. She was gearing herself to leave her office and head down the hall when a masculine voice bellowed, "The hell she doesn't!"

She blinked. Then she reached over and hit the button-lock on her door. Irate student? Irate *parent*? You'd think university kids would fight their own battles, but every semester she had to firmly inform at least one parent that she wasn't going to pass their darling dear-heart simply because they "came from good stock".

"Meg!" the same voice said, much closer, framed by Amy's, "You can't do that!" and then her more strident, "Someone call campus police!"

"Meg," the voice said again, right outside her door. It dropped lower, rubbing like velvet over her spine. "Meg."

She knew that liquid-sin voice. Except he hadn't been able to speak English. She stood so quickly her chair slid back, and fumbled with the lock before yanking the door open and looking up, way up, into black eyes and golden skin, straight black hair falling just past his shoulders.

She stared at Santiago, emotions awhirl, and said the only

thing she could think of. "Since when do you speak English?"

He smiled, his whole face warming. "Since always."

"You bastard!"

"You know him?" Amy asked, still hovering in the hall as if, given a signal, she'd tackle him herself.

"Yeah, it's fine." Meg's answer was quick. She grabbed the sleeve of Santiago's suit—suit?—and dragged him inside. Letting go, she slammed the door, then leaned against it and glared at him.

He *was* wearing a suit. White shirt, no tie, black jacket and pants. His collarbones peeked between the lapels, a glimpse of perfect skin reminding her of the way his flesh moved and shifted over his muscles. The jacket fit him flawlessly, accentuating broad shoulders and narrowing to his trim waist, his slacks falling just so over the tops of his black shoes.

"You speak English *and* you have enough money to wear Armani?" she snapped, fighting down the urge to wrap her arms around him and breathe in his scent.

"It's not Armani," he said, putting his hands in his pockets. "It's—"

"I don't care!" She stopped, one fist pressing against her chest as if she could keep her pounding heart from bursting through. He was here. He was *here*, and she didn't know if she should hope he stayed or knee him for cheating on his wife. She'd always thought she'd knee the guy, but now that she was faced with him—Christ. She'd missed him.

"Meg," he said softly. "Why'd you leave?"

She stared at him. Swallowed. Licked her lips. Finally, she forced out, "You're married." And then, as if that was all she had needed for the pain of seeing him to break through, the lump in her throat gave way to anger. "You're *married* and

Frieda and those boys deserve to have a dad that isn't buggering off to another country! You son of a bitch!"

He dodged her punch, his reflexes faster than human, and stepped in to grab her fist before she could throw another one. "I'm not married," he said, inches from her face. She couldn't just ignore him.

"What do you mean you're not married?" she shouted, not caring who in the department might hear her.

"I'm not married. I've never been married. I only go home a few times a year, and I certainly don't have children in that village."

Meg stared at him. The bottom had dropped out of her world *again*. She needed a vacation. One where she didn't find jaguar-men. "You don't—?"

"No." He shook his head.

"But they told me—"

"They're assholes."

She nodded. That, she could agree with.

"They don't like outsiders. They're afraid of being discovered."

"Oh." He wasn't married. He hadn't cheated on anyone. He pressed close and she became aware of the door against her back, her breasts brushing his chest with every inhalation. His scent surrounded her.

"That's the only reason you left?" he purred, his gaze on her mouth. "Just the wife?"

"That's a damn good reason," Meg protested. He inched closer, nose brushing hers, hand sliding around the back of her neck. "Wait a minute!" She shook her head to clear it and nearly bashed him in the face. "If you don't live in that village, where do you live?"

He smiled. “New York. But I’m willing to change offices and come here.” His smile faltered, and his eyes wouldn’t meet hers. “That is, of course, if you’d like—”

She didn’t wait for him to complete the sentence. Grabbing a fistful of hair, she dragged him down, opening her mouth under his, almost laughing when it took a full second before he responded in kind.

Then he pushed her up against the door, a thigh between her legs, tongue sliding between her lips. After a while they broke apart, panting.

“I’m not done with being mad at you about lying to me,” she said between breaths.

“I never lied to you,” Santiago rumbled, nibbling on her ear.

“You lied by omission. Letting me think you didn’t speak English. Not bothering to tell me you didn’t live in the jungle. Wait—*you’re* the reason the village has rubbing alcohol!”

“I’m one of the ways, yes,” he agreed. His hand slid up over her ribs.

“You do not own a boating business!” she accused.

“I do!” He pulled back just a bit, looking offended. Then he smiled sheepishly. “Well, not boats. Yachts. And I’m only one of the owners.”

He owned a *yachting* business? Meg couldn’t quite wrap her mind around that. “You are *such* a cad,” she growled.

He smiled, body pressing against her. “Cad? Who says cad anymore?”

“Obviously, I do!” She squirmed, biting her lip against squeaking when his fingers found her nipple through her shirt. “Next time you go home, I’m going with you.”

“I’ll take you to all the best ruins,” he agreed, laughing as he kissed her again, and again.

She grinned. "Marry me."

He stopped, pulling back, scowling. "If you would just give me a few weeks, I'll ask you."

"I don't want to wait a few weeks." She shrugged. "Marry me."

"Damn it! That's my line!"

"You're not saying it fast enough. Marry me."

He glowered, then chuckled softly.

"Marry—" Meg began again, only to be forced to a stop when a hand covered her mouth.

"Marry me," Santiago requested. "You'll get to see my annoying, over-protective, lying family a few times a year, and you'll probably find fur in disturbing places. Your cat will hate me, and the food bill will triple in meat products alone." He smiled and removed his hand. "Say yes."

"Since you make it sound *so* appealing," Meg laughed, "yes."

He bent to kiss her, and she pulled back. "How'd you know I have a cat?"

He sighed, leaning his forehead against hers. "Obviously," he muttered to himself, "I'm not doing this seduction thing right."

"How?"

"I can smell him on you." Santiago shrugged.

She thought about that for a long moment. "All right," she said finally. "I can accept all those conditions. As long as there are no barbs."

He blinked at her, slowly and methodically. Like a cat. "No barbs."

She nodded solemnly.

He blinked again. “You’re talking about cat-penis barbs, aren’t you?”

She grinned.

Santiago closed his eyes, a crease appearing between his brows, then finally opened them again. They’d gone yellow. “You know,” he purred, “we’d better check.” Then he grabbed and lifted her, depositing her on the desk.

Meg yelped, wrapping her arms around his neck. Laughing, she helped strip his jacket off and started unbuttoning his shirt.

This was, by far, the best treasure she could ever want.

About the Author

JB has two devoted dogs who faithfully listen to each and every story, and a conure who tells her when she's writing badly. When she isn't cackling maniacally or hatching a new plot, she trains animals and their owners. In the thirty seconds a day when she can't be found on horseback, training dogs, or writing, you can find her tinkering with her website at www.jbmcdonald.com. Or, if you wish to privately encourage her insanity, you can email her at:

Jenna.B.McDonald@gmail.com. She will be forever gleeful.

To stop a killer, would you become one?

Even for Me

© 2008 Taryn Blackthorne

An *On the Prowl* story.

Aislyn used to have a life, a family and a home until a witch on a mission shattered everything in one night with a spell. Now Aislyn is on the run, holed up in Denver, and fighting the Changes that ravage her body and mind while struggling to keep her humanity.

Jackson Havens is a ghost hunter short on cash. All he needs is quick proof that Aislyn is the Ghost Cat Killer, and he can get back to his day job. One pair of handcuffs and a double-crossing employer later, Jackson finds himself bound to the sexy Aislyn—and racing to catch the real killer before someone puts Aislyn down. For good.

Available now in ebook from Samhain Publishing.

Available now in the print anthology On the Prowl *from Samhain Publishing.*

Enjoy the following excerpt from Even for Me...

Whatever power the kid was calling up, the weather was helping. Ozone filled the air up quick. A flash of lightning hit just outside the barn doors, illuminating everything inside clear as day. The kid's shadow looked like a scarecrow but the woman's shadow looked like a cat. A second strike and the woman screamed as if the lightning had hit her nerves. As he watched, the reason for the woman's ankle chains became clear. Her skin shivered, like an ocean wave, and tawny fur rode the top, up to her face. One more flash of lighting and her teeth became fangs, her snout stretched and her pupils elongated and became thin slits that cut through the blue iris of her eye.

She screamed, rage in her face, or at least she tried to. Cougars couldn't roar, but she sure gave her version. Her body arched as the kid looked on, rapt, captured almost, the smoking cigar in her hand seemingly forgotten. The cougar looked at the kid and hissed in hatred. Her body fought and bucked and the wave rolled across her body again, but the fur retreated back down, the face became normal, save for her very cat-like eyes. She turned them on the kid and smiled around the gag.

"NO! You have to Change! Don't you understand? YOU HAVE TO!" The kid lost it, stomping around, and the lightning outside hit the roof. He smelled smoke and knew the old barn had caught. He tried to yell around the gag, but the kid didn't seem interested in him anymore. He tried to kick the stall he was chained to. He pulled and yanked until he couldn't see for the sweat running down into his eyes. Blood dripped off his hands, making them slippery. A witch and a Shifter. He was in it up to his eyeballs this time.

The woman began to scream, clear and loud. He turned just in time to get smacked with a shovel aside the head, stunning him long enough for the kid to pull off his gag and wrap the woman's around his left wrist. She then pulled the cigar up to her lips. He watched the end flare and blinked just before the smoke was blown into his eyes. He coughed and sputtered and gazed up at the kid through a haze that had blue edges to it. The girl smiled at him. She walked across the room to her other prisoner, seemingly unaware that there were now lit pieces of the barn falling all around her, and small fires burning in those stalls that had dried hay in them. She tied his gag to the woman's left wrist and bent over the struggling, cursing woman.

The kid blew smoke into the woman's face and chanted all the way back to the center of the circle. She picked up the bowl of liquid and offered it to the storm outside. A soft rain had begun to accompany the thunder and lightning but he had small hopes that it would put out the fire before at least two of them roasted. The kid put the cigar into the liquid in the bowl and whatever it was caught. The symbols flared and burned on their foreheads and both he and the woman couldn't hold back screeching.

"Iallach a chur ar dhuine rud a dhéanamh," the girl sang and lightning hit the center of the circle, then spread to hit both him and the woman. His body was raised off the ground two feet, every muscle stiff as a board. It felt like he was burning from the inside out, like his nerves were made of acid and caught on fire to boot. No sound could come out of his mouth. He felt, rather than saw that the woman, Aislyn, was in the same position. He had the sudden thought that she'd been running from this kid because this was *the* witch. He'd known that Aislyn was from the East Coast but now he knew she had loved swimming in the ocean, hiking along the rivers, had loved her small apartment in the old town boarding house. Aislyn had loved the smell of a bonfire on the beach with a guitar in her hand and friends gathered around her laughing. She had been so proud of her foster brother Mark when he had graduated and had made the whole family take the day off, closing the gas station/bus stop in their small town. She'd always been there for her foster mother, helping out in the small diner on her days off and in the evenings when she could. Felt how much she'd loved her small town. And it had been taken from her by *the* witch. He also knew she didn't understand. She didn't know what she was now, not truly. He felt something he never thought he would ever feel for a Shifter. Pity.

She hated pity more than anything else, and he knew that too. It made her feel weak, defeated, violated, and defenseless. She'd been stripped of her life for no reason and pity made it worse. He looked over at the Shifter. Their eyes locked. For once he understood what a woman felt because he felt it, truly felt it as if he had a second personality inside him.

"Damn." He looked up at the witch, who smiled.

"Master of the Hunt." The witch threw a handful of herbs at him. Naming him, she was naming him for God's sake. The kid threw a fistful at the woman and whispered, "Mistress Hunter." Then she collapsed, and a beam from the roof fell across her, blocking his view. Although that could have been the thickening smoke burning his eyes. Oh good, he wouldn't die from roasting alive, but smoke inhalation. Yeah.

Looking up, he saw the stall he was cuffed to get licked once, twice, three times with flames from the fallen beam before it caught and started eating away. The heat was getting worse; he could feel the blisters starting on his skin. He started to cough and couldn't stop. He pulled and shouted and yelled, but nothing seemed to be working and he was using up a lot of oxygen he didn't seem to have anymore. He wondered if his family would be able to claim his body or if it would go into an unmarked grave, the same as his older brother's had last year. It was his last thought.

LaVergne, TN USA
22 June 2010
186964LV00008B/13/P

9 781605 041063